Trilogy of Hope
Book One

THE
GARNERING

A novel

R. HILARY ADCOCK

ISBN 978-1-0980-5853-1 (paperback)
ISBN 978-1-0980-5854-8 (hardcover)
ISBN 978-1-0980-5855-5 (digital)

Christian Faith Publishing, Inc.
832 Park Avenue
Meadville, PA 16335
www.christianfaithpublishing.com

Printed in the United States of America

Prologue

Garner: To get or earn something valuable or respected, often with difficulty.

Dictionary of Cambridge

The sudden disappearance of men, women, and children of all ages shocked humanity into chaos and nations into battles for global power...or survival. Those souls that remain on the Earth are left to face the reality that the promises and warnings recorded and preserved in the Bible were true. In this story, the prophesied event is called The Vanishing.

> For in the days before the flood, people were eating and drinking, marrying and giving in marriage, up to the day Noah entered the ark; and they knew nothing about what would happen until the flood came and took them all away. That is how it will be at the coming of the Son of Man. Two men will be in the field; one will be taken and the other left. Two women will be grinding with a hand mill; one will be taken and the other left. (Matthew 24:38–41)

But what hope could there be after The Vanishing? What is to become of those who realize that The Vanishing was of God? And what hope of Heaven could there be for those who pray for forgiveness and salvation after that day?

The Garnering is that hope. To garner is to glean. To glean is to salvage the fallen bits of a harvest that were rejected on harvesting day. Workers are sent into the fields to find and garner that which can be saved. And so, our story begins…

PART ONE
Melek-Gibbor-Rapha

CHAPTER 1

Highway 70 East of Denver, CO

A small group of lost souls gather along the roadway high in the Colorado Rocky Mountains. They huddle together, frightened and confused. Nearby and unseen by human eyes, two Angels of Light watch and wait. They have been dispatched to prepare leaders for redemption and garnering. Their attention and conversation are focused on finding three of the souls.

I SEE A CHOSEN.
HE IS THE LEADER, MELEK.

The man they see stands alone among the trees and scans the high mountain valley that lay below his vantage point. He is tall and trim with red hair and broad shoulders. His long coat hangs from his shoulders to just below the knees of his faded blue jeans.

The massive gray boulder that supports him is the same stone it had been before The Vanishing. The tall pine trees and quaking aspens that surround him are unchanged. The cool mountain air is as sweet and brisk as before The Vanishings. It seems that with nature and the mountain everything is unchanged. Yet, with humanity, nothing is the same.

The sun is low on the western horizon, and the temperature is falling as the tall man in the long coat steps down from the boulder and walks down the gravel embankment along the edge of the highway. An evening mountain breeze brings a chill through his coat, causing his chest and shoulders to tighten.

He stopped and scanned the roadside scene of people and vehicles. There, ahead of him is his red Freightliner and flatbed trailer. To his right is a light gray minivan parked at an awkward angle with one wheel in a shallow ditch. Two women are inside the cab of his big rig and four men stand in front of the truck's tall radiator, gleaning what little heat they could. He pulled the collar of his sand-colored canvas coat up around his neck and continued walking toward the group. The soft fleece lining felt warm and comforting.

The sound of gravel crunching under his boots caused the men to look his way.

"See anything?" The hint of a South Texas drawl flows in his words.

"Nothin' I could tell from up here."

A short stocky man with crew-cut black hair and muscular physique, like that of an amateur body builder, stepped away from the group and approached.

"Name's Bruce. You?"

"Chet, Chet Rawlins."

The stocky man named Bruce looked back at the three men standing in front of the big rig.

"Don't know what happened. Don't know what's goin' on. But I do know this..." He paused and looked sternly at the man he now knows as Chet Rawlins. "We need to help these folks."

Chet looked at the men and then up at the women in his big-rig.

"Look, friend, I'm just passin' through. Not lookin' to get involved."

Bruce took one step closer then responded, "Well, sir, as I see it, these men need help with their vehicle, and those women in your truck need help and protection."

Chet looked down at the scuff marks and mud on his boots. For over a year he had avoided getting involved with anyone. His mother had passed away while he was on the road and he had lost track of his only true friends, fellow pilot Thomas Winslow and architect David Adams. But it was not Tom or David's fault. There had been messages from Tom on Chet's cell phone, but he never returned them. He had worked hard to remain a loaner...and now this.

The Angels of Light see Bruce standing with Chet who they know as Melek, the leader.

THERE STANDS ANOTHER CHOSEN.
HE IS THE WARRIOR, GIBBOR.

Chet looked into the face of the man before him and saw the stern look of military discipline in his eyes.

"You military?" Chet asked.

"Marines. Just retired."

Chet nodded in the direction of his big rig.

"Well, marine, if these people need help, I need your help."

The smile on Bruce's face showed white straight teeth, and his eyes changed from cold steel to warm amity. He stepped forward as he spoke.

"Bruce Coal, United States Marines, retired."

The three men gathered at the truck had been watching the exchange and walked the short distance toward Chet and Bruce. One of them spoke out.

"We need to get off this damn mountain, and for God's sake, we need to find out what happened."

A young man standing behind him spoke out. The words trembled from his downturned mouth.

"What happened? Are you nuts? I'll tell you what happened. Aliens snatched my wife and kids. I don't know why they didn't take me."

He dropped to his knees, put his hands over his face, and wept. The two men with him stepped away as if his emotions might touch them. The man closest Bruce spoke out.

"We need to get out of here!"

He pointed toward the minivan.

"Help us push this thing back on the road."

One of the women watching from inside the big rig wiped condensation from the window with a red shop rag that Chet kept in the door pocket. Snowflakes began to fall, resting on the shoulders of Chet's coat and sticking to his wavy red hair.

Bruce and Chet helped the men rock the minivan back and forth while the driver shifted the transmission from drive to reverse doing his best to match the men's timing. Push number three freed the front wheel from the shallow ditch, and the van rolled onto the pavement. With a simple nod and a wave, they pulled away heading west down the mountain.

Chet and Bruce watched the minivan fade from view in the diminishing visibility as the falling snow swirled on the pavement. Chet turned toward his big rig and rested his hand on Bruce's shoulder.

"You got wheels?"

Bruce pointed across the road to a lifted, black, late model Ford Expedition and answered, "Yes, sir. Over there."

"Pull it over here by my rig. We need to move the women out of my cab."

"Sure thing. Then what?"

Chet started walking toward his truck and trailer.

"I'm gettin' on the CB and find out what in hell happened. It ain't gonna be good news, and truckers have foul mouths. Don't want the ladies to hear it."

As Chet approached the truck, the woman on the driver's side became more animated. The other woman remained huddled against the passenger door clinging to an empty car seat and rocking back and forth. Chet stopped a few feet away and with a hand signal instructed them to open the door. When they did not respond, he shouted, "Come on out."

The deep rumbling sound of the Expedition's engine starting caused Chet to glance over his shoulder. As he did, three small sedans raced by, heading down the mountain road. The snow accumulation had covered the pavement causing the speeding cars to slip and drift as they disappeared from sight. Swirling clouds of snow from their wake drift by as Bruce made a quick U-turn across the road and parked near Chet's big rig.

He rolled down the window and said, "Don't think they're gonna make it far drivin' like that."

Chet did not respond to the remark. Instead he signaled for Bruce to join him. As Bruce walked the sort distance to the big rig, the woman on the driver's side climbed down from the cab.

The Angels of Light standing on each side of Chet see the third soul of the chosen opening the driver's door and climbing out.

THERE SHE IS.

SHE IS THE HEALER, RAPHA.

Bruce ushered her into the Expedition where a stack of three neatly folded military wool blankets rest on the back seat and the heater was blowing on high.

The other woman did not respond to Chet's coaxing. Instead she held the empty car seat and continued to stare blankly ahead while rocking back and forth. He climbed up into the driver's seat intending to rouse her from the trauma-induced trance that held her when suddenly she threw open the passenger door and jumped from the cab. The empty car seat tumbled a few feet scooping up small amounts of snow as it rolled.

She scrambled across the ground toward the car seat. Chet turned and called out to Bruce who was getting the other woman settled into the backseat of the Expedition.

"Hey! She jumped!"

By the time he looked back, she had grabbed up the car seat and was running down the road. Bruce looked toward Chet and then back in the direction Chet was pointing. He saw nothing. She had vanished from sight in the increasing whiteout.

"What?" Bruce asks, looking confused.

Chet pointed in the direction of the fleeing woman and shouted.

"She jumped out of the cab and took off."

Bruce moved around to the driver's side slipping on the snow and hung onto the Expedition's brush guard to steady himself.

"I'll get her!" he shouted as he reached driver's door.

CHAPTER 2

Highway 70 East of Denver, CO

Chet sat watching the black SUV disappear into the white. The Freightliner's seat and backrest felt soothingly familiar. He held the big steering wheel in a two-handed grip as he had done a thousand times before. A chill ran through his body as a gust of cold air passed through the open cab. He quickly pulled the doors closed. Alone again, just him and his truck.

The fleeting moment allowed him to feel a normalcy that he knew would not stay, but being alone in the cab of his red Freightliner allowed him to reflect on the events of the past two hours. Events that made no sense, yet there they were. His gaze was fixed on the instrument panel, and his mind played back memories of his near-death experience.

Chet was unaware of the invisible battle raging around the cab of his truck as the two Angels of Light stood swinging flaming sword in wide arcs. Their presence and power was all it took to stop the Dark Angels from reaching Chet...Melek, as the Angels know him.

His mind drifted into recent memories of events that led into the present.

A run from Denver to Los Angeles with a load of scrap iron on the fifty-three-foot-long flatbed trailer. The heavy cubes had at one time been automobiles and household appliances but were reduced to blocks of twisted metal, broken plastic and shattered glass. The air temperature had dropped and his visibility through the streaked windshield was reduced when he rounded curves that turned west. The speed limit for his gross weight was 20 mph on the 7 percent grade down the west descent,

8.6 miles past the summit and the Eisenhower Tunnel. He had used engine braking to ease the load on the brakes, but the weight of the rig and the pull of gravity pushed the speedometer higher each time he eased off the pedal. The only thing he could see clearly as he rolled around a west turning curve was the speedometer needle at 30 mph and the trailer in the mirrors, drifting toward the centerline. He knew the rig would jackknife if he did not act fast.

It was then that it happened. A big rig with no one in the cab rolled up beside him from behind and tapped the side of his trailer. The impact pushed it back behind his tractor allowing him to regain control. The driverless rig rolled off the road into the canyon as Chet steered down the straightaway and stopped on the side of the road.

Both sides of the road were littered with vehicles. Some were parked with people standing nearby and others had crashed into trees along the road. A small black sedan was parked in front of Chet's truck with a woman kneeling next to the open rear door. Her hands were inside an empty infant car seat. Chet could hear the muffled sound of her wailing and crying as she trembled there, on her knees.

The sound and sight of a pickup truck rolling by with the emergency flashers blinking and horn honking aggressively snapped Chet back to the present with its even stranger reality, the reality he hopes to learn more about on the citizens band radio. He clicked on the CB and pulled the microphone from its hangar on the dashboard.

"Breaker, breaker. This is CR. Anybody out there?"

Static crackled from the speaker, and he adjusted the squelch to clean up the transmission. The voice that came over the radio was garbled, male, and stressed.

"CR...R. ...Mayflower. What's...20?"

"Mayflower, I'm on the 70...8 west of Eisenhower Tunnel. You know what in hell is goin' on?"

There was a long pause, long enough that Chet thought he had lost the signal.

"CR...I'm rollin' out...Dillon...got...on my tail...crazies are tryin'... me over. Goin' west...I get...the 70. Bein' chased by... crazy...of a bit..."

The radio went silent. Chet tried to raise Mayflower, or anyone who would get on, but there was only static. Dillon is a small town at the headwaters of the Dillon Reservoir about six miles further down Highway 70. If he continues west down the mountain, he will pass by the Dillon turnoff. As he thought about what may lay ahead, he reached down and patted the sawed-off shotgun holstered under his seat.

Headlights ahead caught his eye. Bruce's black SUV slowed, made a U-turn across the road and stopped in front of Chet's truck. The big tires made crunching sounds in the snow and muddy pools that were freezing over. Bruce climbed out and walked slowly toward Chet with his hands on top of his head, like a prisoner of war on a forced march. Chet climbed down from the cab and stood by the left saddle tank. When Bruce was close enough to hear, Chet asked, "Find her?"

Bruce stopped, moved his hands to his pants pockets, and slowly shook his head, all without looking up at Chet. His voice carried a tone of frustrated resignation.

"Can't find her. She may have got picked up…don't know. Found the car seat…didn't find her."

He shook his head slowly from side to side then tilted his head back and looked up at Chet. "Have you heard the radio?"

"No. Just the CB."

"There's trouble down the hill. Local radio stations are talkin' about police battles in the streets and military blockades. The country's comin' apart, and it sounds like the cities are locked down."

A woman's voice from behind startled the men causing them to turn around. "We need to talk. I need to know what you plan to do."

She was standing with the military wool blanket wrapped around her shoulders and held there by her hands crossed over her breasts, Indian style. Her raven black hair was pulled back in a ponytail that disappeared down her back under the blanket. There was softness about her facial features, full lips, and high cheekbones. But her brown eyes offset the softness with an intensity that projected a no-nonsense attitude.

Chet could not look away from her beautiful eyes locked onto his. His short trance was interrupted by Bruce's apology.

"I'm sorry. Chet, this is Ruby, Ruby Bliant. She was askin' me what we plan to do and I said I'd let her know when we got back to you."

While Bruce spoke, Ruby's eyes remained locked onto Chet's, making it difficult for him to speak or even think. He stammered through the first few words before recovering from the unexpected affect she had upon him.

"Ruby. Good to meet you. Wish it was under better circumstances."

Her response was quick and blunt. "What do you plan to do?"

Her question was on the problem at hand and no amount of niceties or flirtation was going to distract her. The snow had stopped, leaving the night air crisp and calm with the full moon casting shadows over the white.

Chet pointed toward the heavily loaded flatbed trailer. "First thing I've got to do is drop this trailer."

Bruce jumped into the conversation in an attempt to save Chet from Ruby's interrogational intensity and to offer his plan for the immediate future.

"From what we heard on the radio, we need to stay together." He paused, took a deep breath, and continued. "My cabin is just down the road and I…"

He stopped midsentence when Ruby turned and began to walk away.

"Stop!"

The intensity and authority of his voice caused her to freeze in her tracks.

Bruce pleaded, "Please understand…I only want to help."

Those words eased the fight-or-flight instinct that had overtaken her.

Bruce looked at Chet, and although Ruby was still facing away, he continued. "My wife died a few years ago, and I've been livin' up here alone since then. My place has a mother-in-law quarters she can stay in, and Chet, there are two spare bedrooms. You pick the one you want."

Ruby turned to face the men. "My own apartment?"

Bruce nodded in the affirmative.

"My own bathroom?"

He nodded again.

"My own kitchen?"

Bruce could tell she was getting comfortable with the plan.

"Small, but yes, your own kitchen."

Then Bruce turned to Chet. "What do ya think?"

As he asked the question, Ruby turned and walked back to the Expedition. Chet and Bruce stood in silence with puzzled looks on their faces.

One Angel of Light went with Ruby, known by the Angels as Rapha the healer. The other Angel of Light stayed with Chet and Bruce, known by the Angels as Melek the leader and Gibbor the warrior.

Three Dark Angels lurking in the forest nearby mumbled and hissed amongst themselves and faded away in search of easier targets.

CHAPTER 3

Painted Desert, AZ

Dark Angels roam freely over the face of the earth searching for lost souls to lure and manipulate. One such soul is in their sights as he flees from his captors. Their only limitation would have been the presence of Angels of Light.

STICK TO HIM!

WE'RE ALL OVER HIM.

KEEP IT THAT WAY.

BACK OFF!

LOSE HIM AND YOU WILL PAY.

BACK THE HELL OFF.

The desert sand was still warm in subtle contrast to the cool evening air. The contrails from the military planes patrolling the sky changed from white to pink as the sun slipped below the horizon. Stars were beginning to show, some brighter than others. What appear to be shooting stars were dead satellites that randomly fell from orbit. The news reports called them space junk. Most burn up on the way down, but sometimes pieces of molten metal hit the ground. The bad news is the potential of getting smashed by a piece of the molten debris, but the good news for some is that all the satellites were dying.

GPS satellites misplaced latitude and longitude positions by hundreds of miles, communications satellites broadcast static, and spy satellites were going blind. Without the peering eyes and ears in space, the world was wide open for drifters and escaped convicts.

A full moon was peeking over the mountains to the east as escaped convict Jud Acres hiked across the Painted Desert, the dusty scent of sage rose with each step he took. Night was the best time to travel on foot. The Indian Reservations were quiet. The Indians were asleep or drunk. The rattlesnakes were hidden under rocks, and unless a helicopter came around, no one would see him. He could see vehicle headlights on Interstate 40 three or four miles to the south. He did not understand why so many were stopped with headlight beams pointing in crazy angles, nor did he care. All he cared about was getting as far from Arizona as possible.

Walking alone in the wilderness can cause a person's mind to wander and rethink things. Things like Grand Theft Auto. How in hell did they pin that on him? It was just a limo, and he just wanted to have some fun. The working girls on the Boulevard did flock to it when he cruised by and that almost made it worth it.

Arizona jails had a reputation for being tough, and convict Jud Acres had discovered the stories were true. If it had not been for the trash truck and panic in the prison he would still be there. Lucky for him, the truck driver did not see him slip into the dumpster. And luckier still, the gate guard was distracted by his partner's sudden disappearance. There was a lot of confusion going on, and the time it took for the guards to hit the lights and sound the alarm was enough time for him to ride out with the trash.

A critical part of his escape was to find a change of clothes. Arizona prisoners wear bright pink shirts and baggy pants with wide horizontal black and white stripes. Like a rodeo clown, only not funny. He knew the first thing to do after he got clear of the prison was to get out of his clown suit and sneak out of the truck. While he was lying in the trash pile, he took off the pink shirt and stripped his pants down to his undershorts. He slipped his shoes back on and waited. When the truck stopped at a remote four-way intersection, he jumped out hoping the driver was not looking in the mirrors. He rolled across the pavement and down the gravel apron with rocks and grit digging into his naked back and knees. He lay as flat to the rough ground as he could and watched the trash truck slowly pull away. That was when he saw the backpack and clothes lying on the other side of the road.

A nearly naked man in shoes running across the highway would definitely cause people to look twice. He looked up and down the road to make sure no one was coming then ran to the other side. The clothes were laid out horizontally, and the backpack was underneath like a person lying on his back except there was no person. He dug through the backpack and discovered some dried food and a camel full of water. The clothes were a bit too large, but it was better than being naked in the desert at night. He tossed his prison shoes away and pulled on the hiking boots. They were also too large, but he found another pair of socks in the pack and doubled up.

He figured he could make Gallup, New Mexico, and then grab a ride. His skills were a little rusty, but most anything with a key lock was his in less than two minutes.

And now he was somewhere in the Painted Desert well on his way to freedom. The sound of distant barking caught his attention. It sounded like a bunch of dogs, a pack, running hard. He hoped they were not headed his way. Dogs in packs. Cops in helicopters. All the same to him.

CHAPTER 4

Forest Near Copper Mountain, CO

What Bruce had called a cabin was in fact a stately log home nestled into the forest. The light-brown log walls and the dark-blue eaves along the edge of the dark-green metal roof looked as much part of the forest as the trees themselves. The winding driveway was wide enough for Chet to navigate the big rig tractor without damage to the truck or the trees along the red gravel driveway.

Ruby was first to step out of the vehicles and into the crisp mooring air. She walked a few feet toward the home, stopped, and turned to see Bruce coming toward her.

"Oh my, this is beautiful."

Bruce looked toward the home and smiled.

"Yes, thank you. My wife picked out the colors."

Ruby stepped closer to him. "Beautiful, just beautiful."

Chet joined them.

"Wow, this is some cabin."

*****

Later that evening they met in the Great Room where Bruce had just loaded more logs into the blazing stone fireplace. Earlier he had prepared a steak dinner with salad, fresh vegetables, mashed potatoes, and wine for Ruby. Bruce and Chet enjoyed a beer. The furniture at the fireplace was very rustic and masculine offset by light green and soft yellow cushions his wife had chosen. After everyone was settled and comfortable, Bruce opened the conversation.

"This doesn't seem real. Here we are sittin' by the fire while God knows what's going on down in the valley."

Chet leaned toward the fire and held the palms of his hands closer to the warm glow.

"Don't know what I would do if we hadn't crossed paths, friend."

Ruby, who was sitting between the men, sighed deeply and spoke in a soft whisper. "Yes, thank you."

Bruce stood up and waited to speak until both Ruby and Chet looked his way.

"We need to stay here for a while. We really shouldn't go down the valley till it's safe."

Ruby nodded in agreement.

Bruce then addressed Ruby directly. "My wife wasn't as tall as you, but some of her clothes might fit. Please help yourself to anything you want."

"Oh my, thank you." She then abruptly returned the conversation to problem at hand. "How will we know when it's safe?"

"Radio worked a while ago." Chet added, "CB in the truck."

Ruby stood and moved closer to Bruce. "How long?"

Bruce pondered the question before answering. "Maybe a month or so. Just have to wait and see."

CHAPTER 5

Painted Desert, AZ

Convict Jud Acres's name and description was just one of many thousands listed as escaped or missing. Rap sheets and mug shots were sent to police, sheriffs, highway patrol, and border patrol.

His feet hurt. There was gravel in his boots, he was thirsty, and the sun was coming up. Ahead he could see a two-lane road running north and south. He planned on finding a culvert under the road and sleeping through the day. But he needed water, and the blisters on his heels felt like they were beginning to bleed. As he neared the road, he spotted a black-and-white sign that identified it as Highway 191 and another sign indicating the town of Ganado thirty miles north.

A beat-up pickup truck came into view, rumbling north. Jud decided to risk being seen. He hobbled up the steep gravel road bed and stood facing the oncoming truck. As it came closer, he held out his right hand with his thumb pointing up. The truck was going less than forty-five miles per hour when the old Indian man driving the truck saw Jud. He slowed down and stopped just short of the spot where Jud was standing. Without a spoken word, the old Indian pointed to the pickup bed. Jud nodded in acknowledgment, tossed the backpack into the bed, and climbed in, leaning against the back of the cab. In that position he could see if any cops or helicopters were around and the old Indian would have a hard time seeing his face. Not that he was worried about the old Indian.

He took off his boots, shook out the gravel, and pulled off his socks. The thick cotton material stuck to the bleeding blisters, and the sting of pulling the socks off made him grimace in pain. He mumbled over the rattling noises of the truck.

"I gotta get some wheels."

Settling in with the loose pieces of firewood and rusty junk in the truck bed, he pulled open the backpack and dumped the contents out between his legs. More clothes, a small first aid kit, some bug spray, and a little red book. He stuffed the clothes and bug spray back into the backpack and sat the first aid kit next to his feet. Then he reached down and picked up the red book. The red leather cover was soft, worn, and the gold embossed letters made him chuckle as he read the title out loud.

"The Holy Bible."

Two Dark Angels lurking nearby scurry away in fear.

HE HAS THE BOOK.
HOW IN HELL DID THIS HAPPEN?
GET HIM TO FORGET HE HAS IT.
KEEP HIM FROM OPENING IT.
WHAT IF HE DOES?
WE'LL DISTRACT HIM.

The Bible was compact and he held it one hand. He used his thumb to flip open the cover and found that although the pages were flimsy onion paper, the print was large enough to read. He had never read a Bible. In fact, he never read much of anything except billboards and bar menus. He had heard through prison gossip that Bibles were outlawed, which made them valuable to the right people.

After stuffing the Bible back into the backpack, he zipped open the first aid kit and found a small tube of medicated ointment. He smeared it onto the open sores on his heels. It stung, but the relief of having the boots off and the feel of the morning wind across his face lulled him to sleep. His chin bobbed against his chest with every bump as the old truck slowly lumbered north.

The little red Bible lay safely hidden deep inside in the backpack.

CHAPTER 6

Klagetoh, AZ

Klagetoh, Arizona, is a dusty intersection where a graded gravel road called Indian Route 28 crosses Highway 191. It seemed as though nothing much had changed in Klagetoh since The Vanishing. In truth, there was nothing much there to change. Dust invaded Jud's nostrils as the old pickup truck eased off the pavement and slowed to a stop on the dirt shoulder. Awakened by his own coughing and the jarring of the truck he sat up, twisted from side to side in an attempt to release the knots in his back. Tapping on the rear window of the pickup caught his attention. He looked over his right shoulder to see the old Indian pointing down the gravel road to the west.

"I go there," he said, waiting for Jud's response.

Jud held his hand up gesturing a wait-a-minute signal and quickly pulled on the socks and boots. He tossed the backpack out of the bed on the driver's side and hopped out onto the edge of the pavement. It was midmorning, and the sun burning through the cloudless sky was beginning to heat up everything it touched. He picked up the backpack and stepped closer to the open driver's window.

"Gallup?"

The old Indian pointed east where the gravel road winds across the rolling hills, put the truck in gear, and pulled away. No other words were spoken. The truck turned left onto the westbound gravel road and disappeared in a cloud of dust.

A half hour of deep sleep can recharge a person, especially someone on the run. He looked up and down empty Highway 191 then scanned the horizon to the east. In the distance he could see a small house on the south side of the gravel road. The marginally maintained road to Gallup that passed by the small house was Indian Route 28. He did not know the name of the road, nor did he have a map. If he had a GPS it would not help. Navigation satellites were out of commission and beginning to spin out of orbit. The world was back to paper maps, magnetic compasses, and ground-based radio telemetry. He shrugged the backpack over his shoulder and started walking, following the hard-packed ruts where trucks and cars had crushed the gravel into the earth. His squinting gray eyes remained locked onto the small house.

Twenty minutes later he stood in the dirt driveway facing the small house, looking, waiting for someone to notice him. Nothing. The sun was directly overhead and the heat burned through his matted brown hair.

As he neared the front porch, he noticed a chewed through rope tied to a steel pipe driven into the ground.

He called out. "Anybody home?"

Nothing.

Then he mumbled, "Dog around here somewhere."

The house was sand-colored stucco, weather worn and broken like a hardboiled egg shell. Cracks radiated from the corners of the windows and ran along the wall between the front door and a window that opened onto the porch. Dusty grit covered the porch floor and made scratching sounds as he shuffled his feet and tapped on the bottom of the door with his boot.

"Anybody home?"

No answer.

He grasped the latch and discovered it was unlocked. Hesitantly, he pushed the door open a few inches and looked inside. Tattered living room furniture lined the soiled, beige-colored walls, and a television was cocked into the far corner opposite a faded couch. The television screen was smashed, and a heavy coffee mug lay broken on the floor below it. He looked back over his shoulder toward the road then slipped inside and closed the door. The stale, musty air smelled like urine and wet dogs. He held his hand over his mouth and nose and moved through the small living room into the kitchen where the rank odor was overtaken by the stench of rotten garbage.

Flies buzzed in circles around an open trash can next to the sink. He began to feel sick to his stomach and ran out the back door, gasping in the hot outside air. He had hoped to get food and rest, but it was out of the question.

As he stood on the gravel driveway between the rear of the house and a small shed, he noticed skid marks dug into the dirt and tire tracks leading away from the house. He turned toward the shed and saw another metal post driven into the ground with a rope chewed through.

"Dogs around here somewhere."

As though walking on eggshells, he eased toward the shed hoping that dogs would not jump him. The shed door was held closed by an old splintered two-by-four resting in a pair of rusty steel cradles. He lifted the two-by-four, held it in his right hand like a club, and pulled open the door. Hot dry air laden with the smell of oil and gasoline engulfed him as he stepped through the opening. It took a few seconds for his eyes to adjust from the intense brightness to the dim interior of the shed. As his eyes focus, he saw parked before him an old and obviously mistreated Jeep Wrangler. One headlight was missing, leaving a dark hollow where it had been. The windshield was gone, and in the dim lighting of the shed he could see the engine hood leaning on the wall nearby. Out of the corner of his eye, he spotted a row of four gasoline jerry cans coated with dust and spider webs. He grabbed the nearest can and spun open the cap, accidentally sloshing gasoline over his hands and onto the porous dirt floor.

*****

Engine smoke and the thump of an occasional backfire filled the shed as the old Jeep came to life. Jud set the backpack on the floor on the passenger's side, just ahead of the rails that once held the seat. The little red Bible had worked its way deep into the pack, safely hidden.

He loaded the jerry cans, kicked the tires, and climbed behind the wheel. The sun was getting low and the temperature had fallen into the low seventies as he pulled out of the driveway onto eastbound Indian Route 28. The wind in his face increased as the Jeep struggled past forty miles per hour. Without a windshield and hood, droplets of oil pumping from the engine were caught in the air and blown back, adding to the dirt and grit already caked across his forehead and cheeks. The cooling wind blowing through his shirt and up his sleeves was refreshing, like a waterless shower.

He liked traveling at night and now he had wheels, marginal, but wheels nevertheless. His automotive skills were limited to hot-wiring and driving without headlights, or, in the case of the old Jeep, with one headlight. The thirty or so miles of gravel road and hills between the shed and the town of St. Michaels put Jud and his ride to the test. The worn-out front suspension caused it to wander in and out of the ruts leaving a serpentine track down the road. He needed sleep badly, but keeping the Jeep on the road demanded his full attention.

MESS WITH HIM.
SEND THE HOUNDS AFTER HIM.

He had not noticed the pack of once domesticated dogs that emerged from the scrub brush onto the road until the barking caught his attention. By then, they were in a full run next to the right rear tire. The two larger dogs nipped at the tire and the rest of the pack fell behind, lost in the dust. Had it not been for the barking, he would not have noticed the dog attack. The fear triggered by the sound of barking and the close proximity of the dogs slowly subsided as the old Jeep pulled away from the canine aggressors. He hated dogs and dogs hated him.

CHAPTER 7

St. Michaels, AZ

Jud and the Jeep made it to St. Michaels, Arizona, a poor community inhabited primarily by Native Americans. He was dead tired, and the Jeep was struggling to stay together. The gravel road had become smoother and wider as it neared Arizona Highway 264, and he had not seen another person since leaving the old Indian at Klagetoh.

Decision time. Get on the highway or lay low for a while.

The morning sun shone directly ahead, warming his face and causing him to hold a hand to his forehead as though saluting the sun's arrival. Small houses, barns, and shacks are scattered across the landscape on both sides of the road, and the closer he got to the highway, the more there were. Many appeared to be abandoned with the exception of an occasional dog wandering nearby. He watched for a house without dogs and selected the first one he came upon.

The Jeep kicked up rocks and dust as he turned onto the dirt track that seemed to be the driveway. As the Jeep slowly crept ahead, he watched for activity in the windows and door. Nothing. He parked around the back and turned off the engine. It coughed, kept running, and belched smoke. In frustrated gestures, he turned the ignition key back on and off again, mumbling under his breath.

"What the hell! Shut off!"

If he had mechanical knowledge, he would have known that the severely overheated engine kept running because the cylinders were so hot that residual fuel was igniting and turning the engine backward. In his exhausted state, he finally gave up, turned off the ignition, and walked away, slowly approaching the small rear porch. He knocked on the wood frame of the screen door, unintentionally causing it to bang against the door frame. He waited a few seconds before opening the screen door and reaching for the doorknob. The moment his hand touched the knob the Jeep belched one last backfire and stopped running. He spun around, heart pounding, expecting to see a shotgun pointed at him. It took a few minutes for his pulse to slow and his muscles to relax.

The door was unlocked. He eased it open and called out. "Anybody home?"

Silence.

He waited a few seconds and walked in. The small kitchen had clean plates on a drying rack next to the sink, and he could hear the hum of the refrigerator motor. He ran to it and threw open the door. Cold air, ice, orange juice, iced tea, lunch meat, and a loaf of bread.

Decision made. *Lay low for a while.*

He grabbed the iced tea pitcher and chugged down the cold sweet concoction, letting it overflow onto his chest as he gulped. In relief and excitement, he exclaimed, "Whoa, brain freeze!"

The old house was his deliverance from dust, smoke, thirst, and hunger since his escape. There was food and drink and a bathtub with a shower. He stripped off his gritty, oil-stained, sweat-soaked clothes and started a long shower. The water spraying over his head and ears masked the sounds of the pickup truck pulling up next to the Jeep. Nor did he hear the back door open and a man's voice call out.

"You home? Somebody here?"

The man heard no response but realized the shower was running. He walked cautiously through the house stopping at the partially open bathroom door.

Jud, still unaware of the man's presence, turned off the shower, grabbed a towel, and stepped out of the bathtub. He was looking down at his feet, drying himself and did not see the man standing in the open doorway. When the man saw that the person in the bathroom was not the one who lives there, he shouted, "Who'n hell are you and what'n hell you doin' here!?"

Jud spun around and slipped on the wet vinyl floor, catching himself on the towel bar. The weight of his near fall pulled the towel bar from the wall. It remained gripped in his hand like a club. For seconds that seemed like minutes, the two men stood staring at each other. Jud was naked with a wet towel hanging over his shoulder. The heavyset man in his fifties, dressed like a dirt farmer in bib coveralls and a dirty T-shirt, blocked the doorway.

Jud moved first, reaching for the door to slam it in the man's face. But the heavyset man stepped into the bathroom before Jud could get to the door. In the tussle the heavyset man slipped on the wet floor and fell, hitting his head on the toilet and rolled onto the floor, face up. His eyes are glazed over, his hands quivered, and his head lay at an impossible angle against his left shoulder. Jud wrapped the towel around his waist and knelt down, an arm's length away. He held the towel bar like a stick and poked the man in the ribs. No response. The trembling hands stopped moving, the sound of his breathing stopped, and blood began seeping from his nose and partially open mouth.

*****

Jud waited until nightfall to drag the dead farmer's body outside and bury it in a shallow grave behind the house. During the night he kept the lights off and slept on the living room couch near the front door as a precaution.

In the morning he brewed a pot of coffee, cooked eggs and bacon, and ate sitting at a table for the first time since his escape. After the huge breakfast, it was time to look around the house for clothes and money. He needed both for the next leg to Gallup. The dead farmer's pickup truck parked outside would be his ride.

He turned on the television and cranked the volume up intending to listen as he rummaged through the house. In the bedroom closet he found men and women's clothes, clean, pressed, and neatly hung. The blue jeans and flannel shirts were his size. Running shoes and boots sat on the floor in straight rows. Inside the bottom drawer of the dark wooden five drawer dresser he found a metal strongbox. He broke the small lock, pulled it open, and dumped the contents onto the bed.

A property deed, life insurance papers, a military Purple Heart medal, a small black New Testament Bible, and a plastic freezer bag filled with cash. As he examined the items strewn over the bed, the television broadcast went unheard.

"On the national front…Washington has announced that the United States has joined a multinational commission on religious extremism in response to increased sectarian and related violence. The commission is comprised of prominent leaders from all major world religions and interfaith movements.

"Mobile listening and watching stations have been deployed to aid in the search for the missing and to assist the military and police in regaining order. Interstate highways remain close to the public.

"Now for local news…Search and rescue teams continue to comb the foothills and mountains in hope of determining the whereabouts of the missing. In a related matter, Operation Humanity One is taking applications. Interested female volunteers between the ages of fifteen and thirty-five may contact OHO by texting OHO.ORG."

Jud walked into the living room dressed in new blue jeans, a red-and-white plaid flannel shirt, and white running shoes. He stepped in front of the television and grumbled as he slapped the off button. "Boring!"

He sat on the couch with his back against the padded armrest and his legs stretched out. He dumped the cash from the freezer bag onto his lap and began counting. He felt safe, comfortable, and wealthy as he toys with the paper money and estimates the value.

"One hundred, two hundred, fifty, three hundred fifty, seventy-five, one thousand, two thousand. Two thousand four hundred twenty-five. Not bad."

He looked toward the bedroom.

"…and another Bible. Those gotta be worth somethin' to somebody."

Chapter 8

St. Michaels, AZ

The baseball cap and stooped walking posture made it difficult for Jud to see the young man's face. But the desert camouflage pants, desert brown T-shirt, and military boots were clues that he lived in the house. The contents of the strongbox were still strewn over the bed, and the cash was scattered across the couch cushions.

Jud stood peering through a slit in the living room curtains, his grip tightened on the wooden handle of a twelve-inch kitchen knife held in his right hand. He had three choices: try to escape out the back, hide in the hall closet, or ambush him when he opens the door.

He chose the hall closet and rushed into it just before the front door opened. Keeping his breath as shallow as possible, he watched through a narrow slit between the door and the doorjamb as the young man walked through the living room and into the kitchen. The sounds of chairs sliding around and the softly spoken words of the young man float through the house and into the closet.

"I'm sorry, baby."

Jud could only see a corner of the kitchen. As he slowly pushed the door open a few inches, he saw a chair tumble across the room and heard the sound of the young man's body jerk to a stop at the end of a rope tied to the ceiling fan. He waited until the faint choking sounds subsided then slipped out of the closet and slowly approached the opening into the kitchen. With the knife held before him, he paused and listened. Dead silence.

Jud was unaware of the pain and loss the young man had suffered. On the morning of The Vanishing, he and his young wife had taken a picnic up to a spring-fed oasis high in the hills above their home. They were celebrating his return from the war in China and grabbing some time together before his next deployment.

He had left her by the spring to go collect firewood, and when he returned, she was gone. Her clothes lay in heap on the picnic blanket but she was nowhere in sight. At first, he thought she had stripped off her clothes and was hiding somewhere nearby, playing a sexy game of hide-and-seek. He climbed to a higher vantage point to scan the area and later dredged the shallow water of the spring hoping to at least find her body.

In the letters she had sent him just before he returned home, she confessed that she had asked Jesus into her life and that her life had changed. When he read the letters, he laughed and told his buddies. "The wife's got religion. I'm in deep stink now."

As his futile search wore on, he remembered the cruel laughter and crass jokes that he and his buddies had tossed around the room. After calling her name and searching for days, hope faded and the reality of loss took over. It was the guilt and feelings of indescribable loss that drove him to suicide.

Jud peered around the corner and watched the motionless figure for a full minute. The only movement was a slow back-and-forth rotation of the body as it dangled from the short rope.

Now that the owner was dead, Jud had an opportunity he had not expected. He had shelter, food, and a truck out back when he felt the need to keep going. Until then he would stay hidden from the outside world. He would kick back and enjoy the material offerings of the house. All he needed to make it perfect was a woman.

CHAPTER 9

CAPITIA

A new world power calling itself CAPITIA was culminated within days of The Vanishing. It was made up of three men and three women all of whom had been high-ranking officials in Russia and China. The group named itself CAPITIA...Latin for heads. Except for the members of CAPITIA itself, no one knew their names. Rumors abounded that they meet in remote locations around the world, carried there in stealth vehicles and guarded by formidable security. CAPITIA operated under two entities, One World Order, or OWO, and its sister organization One Humanity One, or OHO. Humanity was discovering that CAPITIA'S control seemed unlimited and growing globally. Radio stations, television, food, medical supplies, and the entire infrastructure of every fallen nation was under CAPITIA'S control.

They imposed their power with a global military and police force combined under the name LEGION whose soldiers were titled Enforcers. It had been determined that peace could only be achieved by immediate enforcement of the following edicts:

1. All governmental leaders of any Democratic or Capitalist nations shall be apprehended and eliminated.
2. All currency shall be issued and controlled by OWO.
3. All commerce shall be controlled by OWO.
4. Implementation and enforcement shall be the responsibility of LEGION.
5. All civilian gatherings shall follow the RULE of 11. Any civilian gatherings greater than eleven persons shall be deemed a violation and punishable by death. Enforcement,

sentencing, and executions shall be the responsibility of LEGION.

6. All religious leaders and spokespersons of all faiths shall teach tolerance and submission to the OWO. Any non-compliant religious leader or spokespersons shall be appre-hended and eliminated.

7. All religious books and writings shall be confiscated and destroyed.

8. All radio and television broadcasts shall be scripted and monitored by OWO.

9. Listening stations shall be controlled and monitored by LEGION.

A secret edict was also sent to the Enforcers of LEGION. It read as follows:

1. All citizens shall be kept tranquil. Any citizens conspiring or participating in unrest shall be apprehended and eliminated.

2. All domestic water systems shall be treated with tranquiliz-ing chemicals supplied and managed by OWO engineers.

3. All Enforcers shall be supplied with mineral and energy enhanced bottled water.

4. All Operation Humanity One, OHO, facilities shall be under the control of CAPITIA.

5. All sentencing and executions shall be performed midday in locations of public gatherings.

6. All human remains of executions and suicides shall be delivered to OHO locations in refrigerated transportation containers identified with the letters OHO in YELLOW, twenty-four inches high.

7. All females of child-bearing age shall be apprehended, sedated, and delivered to OHO BREEDING CENTERS in refrigerated transportation containers identified with the letters OHO in RED, twenty-four inches high.

Enforcement of the edicts was initiated in the cities and over time would spread to smaller communities and rural areas.

Chapter 10

South of Copper Mountain, CO

Three weeks of waiting and listening to static shrouded news reports was enough. Chet, Bruce, and Ruby met for one last breakfast in Bruce's cabin and decided to risk a trip to the valley.

The steady drone of Chet's big rig diesel engine and the low howling of the tires rolling down the mountain road at sixty miles per hour reverberated through the valley, echoing off the rock walls where the highway wound its way south through the Colorado Rockies. Bruce's black Expedition followed close behind, cruising in the near windless comfort behind the trailer-less big rig. Light from the full moon highlighted the silhouette of the foothills against the horizon and cast long shadows of trees and rock outcroppings across the road. Both vehicles coasted effortlessly down the long steady grade, the engines holding back the downward pull toward the valley. They had passed the Dillon turnoff without incident, and with the exception of a few abandoned passenger cars, they had not come upon any traffic. There were no signs of life along their route apart from an occasional deer grazing on grass along the highway's edge.

Ruby had settled into the sleeper behind Chet, lying on top of the bed covers with Bruce's wool blanket draped over her long slender body. She slept with her left arm and hand out from under the blanket. Chet struggled to keep his eyes on the road. Competing emotions rolled over him as he led the small caravan off the mountain to an unknown future. Anger, denial, and guilt faded in and out as the weight of his new responsibility became more apparent. The urgency to get off the mountain charged him with adrenaline-like energy to push on even though he fears that the world is in ruin.

A short time before the world spun into chaos, he had received alarming voicemail messages from his fellow pilot and Christian friend Thomas Winslow. Things about the messages haunted him. There was desperation in Tom's voice and warnings in his words. Chet had not called Tom back. The last message Tom left had what sounded like a riddle that Chet could not understand. He had erased the previous messages but had saved the last message into the memory of his phone. It only took a few key strokes to bring it to life.

"This is Tom. Don't know where you are but this will be my last chance to reach you. Remember, God loves you. When things get strange and people disappear, find hope in the chambers. Col at Vai three five dot three plus three nine plus six. Then one zero six dot three six plus three five plus nine. Under the cross down. God bless and guide you."

The message was a riddle. Pull one or two threads and the rest should come. "Col at Vai" and "under the cross down" meant nothing to him, but the numbers seemed strangely familiar. Yet the answer evaded him. He was snapped back to the present when he saw the flash of Bruce's headlights in his outside mirror followed by a call over the CB. The sound of Bruce's voice filling the cab caused Ruby to stir under the blanket.

"How you doin' up there?"

Chet glanced back toward the sleeper and noticed that Ruby was still asleep curled up in a fetal position, seemingly undisturbed by the noise of the radio. His resolve to protect her was evident by the tone of his voice as he answered Bruce's question.

"Good to go. Let's push on to Pagosa Springs then take a break."

"Sounds good. I must be gettin' a hundred miles a gallon, the needle hasn't moved. How far to Springs?"

Out of habit Chet glanced at his lifeless GPS moving map and a faint thought crossed his mind. It caused him to pause and then it faded away. He pressed the mic button and answered Bruce's question.

"I'm guessn' a hundred, maybe hundred fifty."

"It'll be light by then. Wonder what we'll find?"

Chet sighed deeply and answered in a confident tone, "Don't know, but we can handle it."

Bruce chuckled in response.

"I do like the way you think. BC out."

Chet hung the mic back on the dashboard and looked toward his map case resting behind the passenger's seat. Something was there to solve the riddle, but he still could not put the pieces together.

*****

"I'm hungry!"

Those were Ruby's first words since she climbed into the sleeper. The drone of the engine and gentle rocking of the big truck had lulled her into a deep slumber.

Chet admired her reflection in the rearview mirror. Her hair was a tangled mass, like loosely spun black silk and a hint of child-like vulnerability shone in her sleepy eyes. She was not aware that he could see her, and as she pulled back the wool blanket, her sweater slipped off her shoulders exposing the soft, white skin of her left breast and alluring cleavage. It took all the mental strength he could muster to look away as the words, "Damn, she is beautiful," rolled through his mind. It took several seconds for him to respond to here abrupt statement.

He cleared his throat and whispered, "Me too."

Then he grabbed the CB and radioed Bruce.

"BC. You awake back there?"

The answer came, following a chuckle. "Yeah, sure. I just got up. What's up?"

"I'd like to stretch my legs. What say we pull over for a while?"

Gratitude and relief could be heard in Bruce's voice. "Oh yeah, I'm ready."

"Okay, looks like a turnoff to a campground up ahead. Watch yourself, I'm slowin' down for it."

Bruce had already increased the distance between the Expedition and the big rig.

"Followin' you."

The road to the campground was wide, and the trees had been pruned, leaving room for the tall truck to navigate the circular roadway. Chet pulled over at the second campsite on the right and waited for Bruce.

Ruby climbed into the passenger seat, rolled down the window, and breathed in the crisp, cool mountain air that carried with it the scent of rich compost and pine.

"I need to pee."

Chet opened the driver's door and stepped out onto the soft bark-covered ground. A wooden outhouse marked Men/Women stood a few yards away, and as Chet walked around the front of the truck, he saw Ruby walking briskly toward it wrapped in the wool blanket.

Bruce had parked behind the truck and walked past Chet to a nearby wooden table where he placed three olive drab, sealed plastic packages on the table. He nodded to Chet.

"Come on over. Got us some breakfast."

Ruby came rushing out of the outhouse and shouted.

"Ugh…that's so nasty!"

Both men looked at each other and chuckled. They resisted laughing out loud and had regained composure by the time she reached the table.

Bruce slid one of the packages across the table toward her.

"Breakfast of champions."

She stepped over the bench and sat opposite Bruce. She studied the olive drab object and read its label.

"Scrambled eggs with bacon. You've got to be kidding."

Bruce pulled his military issue Ka-Bar knife out of the belt sheath and slit open the package.

"MRE, Meal-Ready-to-Eat. I've got a few cases of 'em. You never know when the world might turn to crap. Got to be prepared."

When he realized that the intended humor had failed, he quickly grabbed the package and dumped its contents onto the table.

"Everything you need for a hot, high calorie meal is right here. Eggs, bacon, biscuits, jam, powdered fruit juice, toothpicks. Even wet naps."

He waited for her to respond.

She shuffled the brown envelopes around for a few seconds then looked up at him.

"Do we eat this stuff cold?"

"Oh hell no. Watch this!"

With a quick flick of the knife, he opened a cardboard pouch lined in plastic and slipped in the envelope marked Scrambled Eggs and Bacon. Then, just as deftly, he opened a water bottle and poured in a small amount. He smiled and set the pouch aside.

"In a couple minutes you'll have a hot breakfast."

She wrinkled her forehead and asked. "How is that possible?"

"Chemicals."

"In the food?" she snapped.

Bruce shook his head. "Nope, you'll see."

Chet sat silently, watching the exchange. He was familiar with MREs and grateful that they were well stocked in food and bottled water. However, his thoughts have drifted to their unknown future and the damaged world that awaited them down the hill.

THEY WILL STAY HERE FOR A TIME.
WE ARE ON GUARD.

Chet was tired, physically and emotionally, and something prompted him to make a suggestion. "This place feels secure. How about we stay awhile?"

Bruce was busy showing Ruby the proper Marine technique for eating scrambled eggs from a pouch with a plastic spork. Ruby cautiously picked at the hot food deep in the pouch.

Bruce answered, "Works for me. I'll gather some firewood and set up a perimeter."

Chet was not sure what Bruce meant by "set up a perimeter." Later that night he would understand.

CHAPTER 11

Campground North of Pagosa Springs, CO

The glow and heat radiating from hot coals in the center of the fire ring dissipated into the dark cool night of the forest causing the trio to huddle close to the warmth.

COMPLETE THE BOND.
BEGIN WITH RAPHA.

Ruby felt the urge to break the silence. She spoke softly while keeping her eyes fixed on the glowing embers.

"I'm a nurse."

Bruce looked toward her. "How did you end up alone on the road up there?"

She kept her gaze fixed on the fire. "My husband left me."

She brushed away something on her cheek and continued. "I was going to stay with some friends in Denver. When the sky filled with streaks of clouds, I stopped and walked up the hill to look at it. When I got back, my car was gone and you guys were there."

She looked away and rubbed her eyes with her shirt sleeve. "Everything I had was in that car."

Chet felt her sadness and placed his right hand on her left shoulder. "I'm glad we were there when you came back down the hill. I'm sorry about your stuff, but I'm glad you're with us."

She looked at each of them and responded. "Me too."

The heavy emotion in the air made Bruce uncomfortable and prompted him to change the subject. "A nurse? What kind?"

The question helped her control her emotions. She breathed deeply and answered with a tone of pride and authority. "ER... trauma nurse."

"Wow, a nurse! How 'bout that, Chet?"

Bruce poked the coals with a pine branch, causing sparks to float a few feet above the fire and then laid the branch onto the coals.

"Funny how things work out. Here I am hiding in the woods with a trucker and a nurse while the world tries to figure where a bunch of people disappeared off to who knows where."

When Chet and Ruby did not respond, Bruce realized that what he had said was not funny or appropriate. In the hope of fixing the clumsiness of his remark, he continued. "I'm really glad ya'll are with me. Something tells me we need each other."

Chet nodded silently, but Ruby did not respond in word or gesture.

The moment was abruptly interrupted by a vibration in Bruce's shirt pocket and the sound of a large branch breaking not far away. Bruce pulled a small flat device the size of a cell phone from his shirt pocket and studied the images it showed.

"We've got a big cat out that way." He pointed into the darkness and continued. "And some elk over there," pointing in the opposite direction.

"Looks like we're in the middle. What say we call it a night and get in the trucks?"

Chet turned to Bruce, pointed to the device in Bruce's hand, and asked, "What is that?"

Bruce smiled and answered, "I set up a MAIP. It's one of my marine toys."

"An MA what?" Chet asked.

"A motion alarm infrared perimeter. MAIP."

Then he smiled, turned, and walked toward the Expedition. "Night all."

The unseen Angels of Light stationed themselves around the trucks.

CHAPTER 12

North of Pagosa Spings, CO

Hard braking in a tractor without a trailer is a rough ride. The rear suspension recoils causing the eight rear tires to hop violently, leaving short black skid marks on the pavement, like black dashes on a piece of gray paper.

The Expedition swerved left missing the big rig by inches and came to a stop in the center of the road. The limited visibility caused by the morning haze had nearly taken its toll.

In the road ahead stood a tall muscular man straddling the centerline, hands on his hips, frozen in place like a misplaced life-sized statue.

Bruce was out of the Expedition and signaling Chet to stay in the truck before he could open the door. He rolled down the window intending to speak, but Bruce held up his right hand in a stop signal.

"Stay there. I'll handle this."

Ruby had been tossed off the bunk onto the floor. She recovered and climbed into the passenger seat. They watched cautiously as the drama unfolded. In the short time it had taken Chet to look toward Ruby and back at the man in the road, Bruce was standing less than three feet from the man. He had intentionally placed himself between the muscular man and the trucks. They stood face-to-face eyes locked.

Bruce spoke first, "You all right?"

Except for a twitching under his left eye and a subtle shift in weight to his left foot, he did not respond. His sweat-stained blue denim shirt with the sleeves, cut off at the shoulders, revealed snake-like tattoos running from his upper arms under the shirt and onto his neck. The prison-cut physical build and expressionless face confirmed to Bruce that the man was an imminent threat.

The muscular man reached behind his back and brought forward a Glock 9mm pistol, pointing it directly at Bruce's stomach.

"No, but I'm gonna be. I'm taking the fancy black truck."

Then he nodded toward the big rig where Ruby was watching through the windshield.

"And the bitch."

Unseen Angels of Light stood by the trucks with flaming swords drawn while hissing sounds emitted from the nearby Dark Angels whose destructive plan was about to be quenched.

One point eight seconds! Step-grab-pull-twist-BANG!

In less than two seconds, the muscular assailant was overpowered and lying on the pavement, eyes open, staring blankly at the sky. The sound from the pistol's report grew weaker with each returning echo, symbolic of the wasted life that faded away on the pavement. The only movement was blood seeping from under the body and pooling near his tattooed neck. Bruce remained in a ridged stance, feet apart, with the dead man's gun in two-handed grip, aimed at the dying man's chest.

Chet and Ruby rushed out of the truck and ran to Bruce's side. He glanced at Chet then back at the bleeding corpse.

"Had to do it. No choice."

Then he lowered the pistol to his side and sighed deeply.

Ruby knelt down and with a hand movement closed the dead man's eyes.

Chet placed his hand on Bruce's shoulder. "How did you do that?"

Bruce sighed deeply again, as if the exhaled air would purge the event from within. Then he answered in a low voice. "Krav Maga."

*****

The summit at Wolf Creek Pass was behind them and twenty miles of downhill switchbacks to Pagosa Springs lay ahead. They had buried the assailant on the side of the road and continued on without a word spoken.

Chet wanted to know more about Krav Maga.

Ruby wanted to know more about Bruce.

And Bruce was searching for news on the radio. He eventually found a station broadcasting out of Pagosa Springs.

"A spokesman for OHO has advised everyone to remain in their communities until further notice. Food, bottled water, and medical supplies are being flown into Denver, Grand Junction, and Pueblo. Supplies will be distributed by truck and helicopter to smaller communities within the next five to seven days. Information will be updated every six hours, on the hour."

The news prompted him to contact Chet on the CB. They had agreed to use initials rather than names, to keep the messages short and avoid broadcasting anything that might give away their location.

"CR, CR."

Chet quickly responded. "Go."

"News on nine eight point six, FM local."

Chet answered, "Will listen and call back. CR out."

Chet dialed in the station.

"...has informed local police that the 160 to Farmington is closed to non-essential trucks, cars with travel trailers, and RVs. Local area residents in passenger cars and supply trucks with military escorts will be permitted. All Interstate Highways are closed to the public until further notice."

Ruby, who was curled up in the passenger's seat, spoke up.

"Sounds like we may not get to Farmington in this truck."

It was the first time she had spoken for over an hour. He looked toward her, cracked a smile, and said, "I'm not givin' up my truck... we'll work somethin' out."

She turned toward the side window without responding. Watching the trees and boulders sliding past reminded her of the rocky marriage that had died days before The Vanishing. Chet and Bruce were the first men she had been close to since then, and she felt safe with them.

The visual memory of seeing her stretched out in the bunk with her sweater gapped slightly opened played in Chet's head like a looping video. He wanted to say something, anything, but all he could do was chuckle.

She turned to him and asked, "What's funny?"

"Oh, nothing, Just enjoyin' havin' you along."

He wanted to say more but his mind struggled with self-criticism. *Oh god, what a stupid thing to say. What was I thinking? Oh, wait, I wasn't thinking!*

She pointed ahead and saved him with another question. "Can we stop at the river?"

It took all his strength to answer. The image in his head of her standing waist deep in clear flowing water, beckoning him to join her, stifled his words.

"You all right?"

His face turned red as he answered, "Sorry, had my mind somewhere else. Let me check with Bruce."

He cleared his throat and took a deep breath. "BC, BC."

"Go"

"Gonna stop in ten."

"Follow'n' you."

Chet glanced toward Ruby and nodded.

"That's a yes."

CHAPTER 13

Pagosa Springs, CO

At first glance the sights of people walking along the sidewalks, roaming in and out of stores, and carrying groceries to their cars might make one believe that The Vanishing had never happened, but there was a strangeness to the scene. The people looked old and moved abnormally slow…and something was missing. There were no children or women under thirty, which gave the streets of Pagosa Springs a surreal and staged look, like a B-rated horror film.

Chet parked the big rig on the far end of a large parking lot next to the river, and Bruce had driven across the bridge into town in search of fuel for the Expedition.

Chet and Ruby walked down a trail to the riverbank. He watched as Ruby rushed to the river's edge, tossing a rhetorical question over her shoulder as she ran.

"I need a bath! Do we have to wait for Bruce to get back?"

Her childlike behavior and the already answered question caused him to smile and slowly shake his head.

"You're a big girl. Do what ya want. I'll be right here."

Dark Angels lurking in the forest on the opposite bank of the river saw Ruby running toward the water.

WHOA, LOOK OVER THERE.
GET THE HUNTERS.

Chet eased himself down onto the bark and pine needle-covered ground and leaned back against a boulder on the edge of the trail. It felt good to be out of the driver's seat, and it felt even better to be there with her. He watched as she slipped off her shoes, rolled up her pant legs, and tiptoed into a shallow pool along the riverbank.

The sound of a male voice coming from upstream caused her to grab her shoes and run back to Chet.

"Hey! We got a Breeder down there. Good-lookin' one!"

Chet also heard the voice and was on his feet holding his hand out toward her and whispered, "Quick, let's get back to the truck."

They walk briskly and quietly hand in hand up the trail and across the pavement to the waiting big rig. Chet helped her climb in on the driver's side and then slid the shotgun from the holster under the seat. She looked down at him from the cab with a look of uncertainty.

"What do we do?"

"Get back in the sleeper and stay out of sight."

She quickly obeyed and was in the sleeper before he closed and locked the door. He walked around to the front of the big rig and leaned against the left front fender. From that position he could see the trailhead and forest along the river. He cocked the shotgun, held it at his waist, and flipped off the safety.

Two men came out of the forest and one from the trail. All three were dressed in camouflaged hunting pants and jackets and carrying rifles. When they saw the shotgun, they stopped and shouted.

"You see a woman go by here? Tall...long black hair."

Chet stood to his full six-foot-two-inch height and slowly raised the barrel of the shotgun toward them, holding it at his side.

"You boys need to move along."

The men stood facing Chet. The tall one in the middle nodded to the other two and they stepped a few feet away. Unless Chet's reflexes were quick, he would not be able to get buckshot into all of them.

The sound of Bruce's Expedition careening across the parking lot toward them caused them step back and lift their rifles to their shoulders. As they watched, the Expedition lurched to a stop with the driver's door facing them. Bruce's left arm was sticking out of the window with the Glock 9mm in his hand, aimed at the guy closest to him.

Chet repeated the instructions.

"Like I said, you boys need to move on. Lay the rifles on the ground and get the hell outta here."

The tall guy in the middle slowly bent over and gently laid the rifle at his feet. Then he nodded to the other two who reluctantly obey.

Bruce climbed out of the Expedition and stood next to the front fender, facing their flank. The authority in his voice caused them to look toward him in unison.

"Now back away. Slow."

As the men backed away, Chet and Bruce moved forward and stopped at the rifles lying on the pavement. The men continued their retreat until they reached the edge of the forest where they stopped. The tall guy raised his right hand toward them with his index finger aimed at Chet.

"This ain't over!"

Bruce looked toward Chet and waited for him to respond.

Chet raised the shotgun to his shoulder, aiming at the tall guy's chest. Bruce raised the Glock in a two-handed grip and aimed at the forehead of the guy on the right.

In verbal response to the pompous threat, Chet growled three words. "It can be!"

The men turned and ran into the forest shouting obscenities and threats.

Bruce stood firm keeping watch on the forest where the men had fled. Chet gathered up the rifles. He walked back to the truck, opened the driver's side saddle box, and prepared to pack the rifles in among his tools and blankets. He examined the rifles and called out to Bruce. "Check this out!"

Bruce made one last visual scan of the forest and joined Chet at the truck.

Ruby rolled down the driver's side window and watched.

"What you got?" Bruce asked.

Chet held one of the rifles out, cradled in both hands.

"It's a dart gun. Three of 'em.

Bruce took the piece and pulled back the bolt, ejecting a projectile. He picked it up and after a quick inspection said, "Tranquilizer dart. What the hell?"

Ruby answered the question. "I'm afraid I know what they want."

She paused, shook her head slowly, and continued. "I wasn't sure I heard correctly, but now I think I know."

Her voice trembled. "They called me a 'breeder.' I think they're hunting women and taking them alive."

Chet looked at Bruce then back at Ruby.

"Breeder? You mean like livestock?"

She cocked her head to one side and answered, "Remember the woman on the mountain with the empty car seat?"

The men nodded and then she looked at Bruce and asked, "Did you see any children in town?"

Bruce looked across the river toward town and answered, "Nope, didn't see any kids in town. None."

"So, their collecting women to breed them?" Chet asked in a tone of disbelief.

Ruby nodded and Bruce responded, "Sure looks that way."

Chet placed the rifles into the saddle box, turned to Bruce, and asked, "Did you see a truck stop?"

"Didn't see a truck stop, but I did see some big rigs comin' and goin' from a warehouse on the west side to town. Just past the station where I fueled up. A guy there said that was where the big rigs were gettin' their fuel and loads."

He paused and pulled out his wallet.

"And it looks like our money won't be good for much longer. The guy took it for the fuel but said we need to exchange it for the new government money cards."

Chet reached over and tapped the big rigs saddle tank. His action got Bruce and Ruby's attention.

"I've got an idea. Remember we heard on the radio that only trucks with loads and military were allowed on the highway to Gallup?"

Bruce and Ruby waited for him to finish telling his idea.

"Let's head over there and see if we can get a trailer. Cause if we get a trailer, we get fuel."

He nodded toward Bruce. "You have military ID?"

Bruce tapped the back pocket of his faded jeans. "Yup, I do. And you know what? This just might work."

Chet looked toward Ruby whose only response was a nod of her head, which caused a long lock of her hair to fall over her left shoulder. Chet took a few seconds to recover from the rush he felt as her image played in his mind.

Bruce broke the silence with his response.

"Let's roll."

CHAPTER 14

Pagosa Springs, CO

Ruby stayed hidden in the sleeper compartment of the big rig as they merge in behind two trucks traveling west and cross the bridge into town. Bruce followed close behind in the Expedition. When they approached the warehouse driveway, one of the two trucks they were following turned into the yard and the other continued west. Chet followed the truck into the warehouse yard and was flagged down by a potbellied workman wearing a yellow lab coat and a brown baseball cap.

Ruby pulled the sleeper curtain closed and whispered, "Are you sure about this?"

Chet answered while keeping his eyes on the approaching man, "Don't worry, this will work. Just stay out of sight."

As the man neared the truck, Chet rolled down his window and waited for him to speak first.

"You here for a load?"

Chet leaned out the window to prevent the man from seeing into the cab. "Yep."

"Pull over there and park by that white building. Dispatch is inside on the right."

Chet followed the instructions, parked, climbed out of the cab, and locked the door. He walked the short distance to the dispatch office, ascended the wooden steps, and stopped on the landing before entering. From that vantage point he could see the Expedition parked along the road outside the yard. He nodded in that direction assuming Bruce could see him. Knowing that his able-bodied friend was nearby calmed his nerves. He took a deep breath, turned, and entered the building.

Immediately on his right was a small counter with a security glass window, like the check-in window of a motel in a high-risk neighborhood. He was reading the collage of notes, instructions, and warnings stuck to the bulletin board next to the check-in window when a skinny gray-haired woman in her sixties slid open the window.

"You here for the OHO trailer to Gallup?"

Chet was speechless for a few seconds, confused by the question and surprised by the opportunity.

"Honey, I'm busy as hell. I can see your truck from here and you ain't got a trailer. Are you the replacement?"

Chet paused long enough to process her question. *Replacement, no trailer, Gallup.*

"Uh, yeah, I guess I am."

She shook her head slowly from side to side then looked up at Chet.

"Truckers! You drifters gonna be the end of me."

She pulled a large white envelope from a stack of papers on her desk and leaned toward him. The wrinkled folds of loose skin on her thin neck jiggled as she spoke and patted the envelope.

"I was supposed to have this load outta here six hours ago, but the tractor we hired broke down somewheres. I don't care if he sent you or you just got lucky. Do you want the job or not?"

Chet did not hesitate to answer. "Yeah, I'll take it."

He held out his hand for the envelope. She picked up a rubber stamp and slammed it onto the face of the envelope.

"Take this and wait by your truck. One of the yard boys will get you loaded. When you're done come back in here. I'll log you out when your escort shows up."

The radio news he had heard earlier had said that supply trucks were traveling with military escorts.

"Oh, I got my guy with me already."

She looked up with an expression of surprise. "Military?"

"Yeah."

She rummaged around the desk and found a blank form. "He needs to fill this out and file it with me before you leave."

Chet smiled. "No problem."

As he walked outside, he read the red ink stamp on the envelope.

<u>EXPEDITE</u>
Fuel card-ammo card-interstate pass

He climbed into the cab and heard Ruby whisper from behind the curtain. "We okay?"

He answered while reaching for the CB, "Yeah, we got lucky."

He pressed the mic button. "BC…BC."

The radio crackled back.

"Go."

"Come to me. Over."

"Gate?"

"Got ya covered. CR out."

Chet whispered to Ruby as he slowly climbed down from the cab, "Gettin' Bruce, sit tight."

He did not hear her soft barely audible "Okay" as he closed and locked the door. The gate and roving workman in the yellow lab coat were a few yards away from Chet when the Expedition pulled into the yard. The workman was waving down the Expedition with exaggerated arm movements. Bruce stopped and waited.

Chet called out, causing the workman to stop and turn in his direction, "He's with me!"

As he spoke, he held the white envelope in the air.

*****

A yard-tug slowly rolled a gleaming white box trailer into position behind the fifth wheel of Chet's big rig. Chet walked around the trailer and saw the tall red letters painted on both sides:

<u>OHO</u>
Operation Humanity One

He continued the visual inspection and stopped at the rear doors where he discovered plastic seals placed over the locks on the doors. Hanging from the locks were warning labels and another plastic seal was stuck across the joint between the doors.

PROPERTY OF OHO
UNAUTHOREZED ACCESS PUNISHABLE BY DEATH

Bruce approached holding an olive-drab-colored file folder under his arm.

"We're all set. I got fuel cards for the Expedition, ammo for the Glock, and a map showing locations where convoys have been ambushed over the past two weeks."

He continued with a gleam in his eye. "Looks like this will be an interesting trip."

Chet nodded toward the rear doors. "And it looks like we're not supposed to know what we're haulin' in the reefer."

Bruce looked puzzled. "The what?"

"Reefer…refrigerated trailer for haulin' meat and frozen stuff."

The yardman guided the tug the last few inches and disconnected the tug. He nodded toward Chet. "Get hooked up and meet me at the gate, pronto. This load is behind schedule."

Ruby watched from inside the sleeper as Chet connected the power and air hoses and Bruce pulled the Expedition alongside the big rig. He saw her peeking from the sleeper window, and when she looked in his direction, he winked. Suddenly aware that she could be seen from outside, she quickly slipped back away from the window and gently closed the gap in the curtain.

As Chet climbed into the cab, he heard her whispered prayer. "God. Please get us out of here."

That was the first time Chet had heard anyone pray since before The Vanishing, and that made him think about the voice message from Tom and the riddle.

CHAPTER 15

West of Pagosa Springs, CO

For Jud it was a good day.

He had money, the heater in the truck blows warm air, the gas tank is full, and the sun would set before he reached the paved road. He watched in the rearview mirror as the house grew smaller and faded from view. The graded road wound through the hilly pinyon pine forest, and overhead a solid overcast of dark clouds blocked the sky. Rain began to fall, and the red clay road surface grew slippery.

As he rounded a curve, he saw her. Dark skinned, thin, dressed in green hospital scrubs, and barefoot. He pulled over and drove slowly toward her. As the rain intensified, the large red boulder she was sitting on darkened to the color of dried blood. Her green hospital scrubs clung to her shoulders and small breasts like a heavy wet T-shirt.

He stopped a few yards away and waited for her to look up. She did not. Instead, she sat with her hands under her thin thighs and her eyes fixed on the wet ground below her feet. He stepped out of the truck and walked slowly toward her. The red mud clung to his shoes.

Suddenly she looked toward him and screamed.

"Get away. I won't go back!"

The sudden reaction startled him, causing him to stop in his tracks, slip, and fall backward. He landed butt-first in the mud with both hands mashed into the mud at his sides. For a few seconds they both sat in the pouring rain staring at each other.

"Look, girly," he snarled from his wet and muddy sitting position. "I just stopped to see if you want a ride."

Unfortunately, that was not the whole truth. He had not had a woman for over ten months and he hoped she would be his travel companion. It would help his cover and maybe he would get lucky.

"You're not from OHO?"

He cautiously stood back to his feet and wiped his muddy hands on his soaked blue jeans.

"O…what?"

She slid off the rock and stepped closer to him.

"You don't know what OHO is? Really?"

He shook his head and wiped his forehead with the back of his left hand. As he spoke, he noticed her shoulders and arms shivering.

"Really! Now can we get in the truck?"

He turned and walked back to the truck.

She followed.

*****

The pickup truck with Jud and the girl turned off the graded road onto the pavement of southbound Highway 491. In his clumsy male chauvinist fashion, Jud was persistent in trying to get the girl loosened up.

"So…you look like you got Indian blood in that sweet body."

She scooted up against the passenger door creating as much space between them as possible and did not answer.

"That was meant to be a compliment, girly. Guess it didn't work, so how about telling me how you ended up on the side of the road."

She sat in silence staring out the passenger's window. He reached over and put his hand on her leg just above the knee. She spun around, pushed his hand away, and released her seat belt.

"Let me out. Jesus doesn't want you to touch me."

"Jesus!" Jud exclaimed.

She folded her hands, rested them on her lap, and looked straight ahead as she spoke.

"Yes, Jesus. The Bible says He loves me and He will protect me. Now stop and let me out."

PROTECT HER.
THE CHOSEN ARE NEAR.

One of the Angels of Light swept his sword over the rear of the truck. The report of the tire exploding was followed by a swerve to the right. Jud yanked the wheel to the left and locked the brakes. The pickup truck continued to skid and slammed to a stop when the front wheels fell into a concrete drainage ditch. The girl was thrown against the dashboard and slumped on the floor, unconscious.

Jud had braced for the impact, but when the steering wheel airbag deployed, it slammed onto his face like a prizefighter's punch and broke his nose. Blood dripped from his face and onto his pants.

Steam coming from under the hood and engine oil flowing under the truck was evidence that the pickup truck was damaged beyond repair. The passenger's door had popped open but the driver's door was jammed shut. He forced it open with his shoulder and climbed out. At first, he could not keep his balance and held onto the mirror to steady himself.

He looked back into the cab and saw the girl on the floor. The pant leg of her hospital scrubs was torn open from below the knee to the waist band exposing her thin smooth thigh and hip. He looked lustfully at the soft skin and felt the arousal and blood flow of sexual fire burning in his blood-stained pants. With a glance around to see if they were alone, he slowly walked around the back of the truck to her side. There was no need to rush; it had been a long time since he got laid, and he intended to savor every second.

From where he stood, he could see her small waist and the soft swelling of her breasts where her scrub's top was pulled up and wedged against the seat. The fire in his loins intensified, bordering on pain.

They had been driving for a full day, and the only conversation had been about Jesus loving her and protecting her, and now she was barely conscious, exposed and helpless. It looked like she was his for the taking. He reached through the door opening and grasped her shoulders. By twisting and pulling he was able to free her and drag her onto the dirt next to the truck. She was mumbling incoherently but he was not listening. Blood from his nose dripped down onto his hands as he loosened his belt and unzipped his pants.

The sound of a big rig slowing under engine braking caught his attention. He looked up the road and saw an approaching red truck and white box trailer.

Chapter 16

West of Pagosa Springs, CO

Chet's big rig with Bruce's Expedition following close behind approached the crest of a hill heading south on Highway 491. Ruby was attentively watching the road ahead looking for roadblocks or gangs. So far, the trip had been uneventful.

"Something is not right."

Chet glanced at Ruby and asked, "What do you mean?"

"I don't know. I just feel like something is wrong. I can't explain it."

They crested the hill, and the big rig began to pick up speed. Chet pressed the engine braking control to slow the descent. When Bruce heard the deep growling hum of the diesel he eased back, putting more distance between him and the box trailer. He watched for the brake lights and picked up the CB.

"CR, CR."

Chet grabbed the mic and answered, "Go."

"Long hill? I can't see from back here."

Chet responded, "Yeah, and it looks like we got a wreck about a half mile ahead. I'm pullin' over."

Bruce answered back, "I'm commin' around. We clear?"

"Clear."

Bruce eased left, accelerated, and passed the big rig. When he was well ahead of the truck he eased over and slowed to a stop on the dirt shoulder. Chet followed and stopped behind the Expedition.

They had stopped close enough to see a skinny man standing next to a pickup truck with its nose partially embedded in a ditch. They did not see the girl lying on the ground next to him.

Bruce had rigged a holster for the Glock on the inside face of the driver's door. He grabbed the pistol and stepped out onto the edge of the roadway. He looked back at Chet and, with a nod, signaled him to come.

Chet climbed down from the cab with his shotgun in hand and walked toward Bruce. "Not sure. Could be a setup."

Bruce agreed with another nod and said, "How about you look around to make sure we're not getting flanked and I'll get closer."

Chet agreed.

Bruce walked cautiously toward the wrecked pickup, and Chet scanned the areas around their trucks. Ruby climbed out of the cab and joined Chet.

"What do you think?" she asked.

"Don't know yet. Bruce is getting a closer look."

They heard Bruce call out to the man by the wrecked pickup. "You hurt?"

The skinny man had been watching the vehicles approach and had zipped his pants and fixed his belt before they got too close. He pointed to the ground next to the pickup truck.

"No, but my friend here is."

Bruce quickly glanced down at the girl then back at him and asked, "You armed?"

The skinny man held his arms out to his side and answered, "Nope, but I see you are."

"Name?" Bruce demanded.

"Jud."

"Who's that on the ground?"

"Hitcher I picked up a few miles back."

With his eyes locked on the man named Jud, Bruce gave a hand signal over his shoulder. Chet and Ruby joined him.

When Ruby was close enough to see the girl on the ground, she immediately rushed past them. Bruce and Chet looked at each other and quickly caught up with her. Jud remained standing with his arms spread out as he watched the tall slender woman running toward him. His eyes were locked onto the undulating movements of her breasts that telegraphed through her white T-shirt as she ran.

When the trio reached him, he smiled.

"Glad you came along. I was just getting' ready to do her…er, do something for her."

Ruby moved past him and knelt on the ground next to the girl.

"Chet, do you have a first aid kit?"

He nodded in the affirmative.

"Please go get it."

While waiting for Chet to return, Ruby checked the girl's pulse and did a quick visual examination for injuries.

"She is bruised but no broken bones."

Chet arrived and knelt down next to her.

"Here you go."

She snapped the latches and flipped open the lid revealing comprehensive first aid materials.

"You have a serious doctor kit here, Chet."

"Yeah, a person never knows when you need one."

"If there is a flashlight in there, get it for me."

He handed her a small LED flashlight. She gently held the girl's eyelids open and, with a sweeping motion, waved the bright light over the girl's eyes.

"She has a concussion. Help me move her to the truck."

Chet lifted her and cradled her in his arms, like a father carrying a small child. Ruby held her head as they walked slowly to the big rig.

Jud had not spoken and had lowered his hands to his side. When he was sure Bruce was not looking, he checked his zipper.

"So. Any chance you can give me a ride to Gallup? This truck is done."

Bruce patted him down for weapons and, based on the scrawny build, determined he was probably not a threat. At least not one Bruce was worried about. He tossed the answer over his shoulder as he turned and walked back to the Expedition.

"You ride with me."

PART TWO
Redeemers Clan

CHAPTER 17

Gallup, NM

Interstate 40 runs along the northern edge of Gallup, New Mexico, bypassing the small town completely except for three off-ramps: one on the east side of town, one in the center of town at Ford Street, and one on the west at Highway 491. On the day after The Vanishing, the military took control of the interstates, closing the ramps with concrete barriers and patrolling the highways in armed vehicles.

It had been the intent of the Federal Highway Act of 1956 to create the Interstate Highway System for military transport in case of an attack or national emergency. In Capitia's view, The Vanishing qualified as both.

Back in the days before the interstate was built, all the east and westbound traffic passed through town on Highway 66, and so it was again. Cars, trucks, motorhomes, and motorcycles roared through town, most looking for fuel or food, others looking for trouble. Looting and panic had destroyed most of the outlying commercial district, but the heart of town was spared.

The three highways that surrounded downtown connect in a triangle and create a defensible perimeter, like a circle of wagons ready to fend off an attack. Safely surrounded by the paved perimeter, downtown Gallup had everything it needed for the twelve thousand men and women remaining after The Vanishing. There were no children. Just as happened all over the world…they had vanished.

Anger and apprehension hung in the air like an invisible stench. Several men and women had committed suicide in their homes. Others had driven away with the panicked masses. For those who stayed a bond of survival united them into an organized militia. At three strategic locations, the people stood behind roadblocks built of trucks and cars across the main roads into town. One roadblock at the intersection on the south side of the interstate where Highway 491 met West Aztec Avenue. Another to the east across old Highway 66 at Boardman Drive. And the third at the southern end of town where Highway 602 met South 2nd Street. Armed with hunting rifles, shotguns, handguns, and compound hunting bows, the men and women sentinels of Gallup watched and waited.

As the town of Gallup watched, military convoys intermingled with big rigs pulling refrigerated box trailers branded with OHO logos flowed past on the interstate. The citizens of Gallup had no idea what the box trailers contained.

CHAPTER 18

Highway 461 North of Gallup, NM

Dusk had slipped into a moonless night.

The injured girl was asleep in the bunk, and Ruby was curled up in the passenger seat with her knees pulled up to her breasts. Her arms were wrapped around her folded legs, holding them in place. She looked toward Chet and asked, "You getting tired?"

Chet sighed deeply and glanced across the cab in her direction. The glow of the truck's instrument panel illuminated their faces.

"Not too bad. You look ready for some shut-eye."

She rubbed her eyes and confessed, "I sure would like to lie down awhile."

Chet nodded. "No safe place to stop around here. We need to keep rollin' till Gallup."

Bruce had moved into the lead position at nightfall. The taillights of his Expedition shone fifty yards ahead.

The Angels of Light following close by received orders.

ALERT THE REDEEMERS INTO ACTION.
YES, LORD.

Chet picked up the mic. "BC, BC."

"Go."

"How you doin' up there?"

"I'm good. Passenger's asleep in the back. We still pushin' to Gallup?"

"Yeah, be best. You up for it?"

Bruce hesitated before answering. "Chet, we've got some lights up ahead. I'm slowin' down."

Chet eased off the accelerator.

"I see it. Hate to stop out here in the pitch dark, but we better."

The brake lights of Bruce's Expedition came on.

"Stay close behind me and I'll find a spot to pull us over."

Ruby had come out of her drowsy state. "What do you think it is?"

Chet reached over and placed his hand on her knee in an attempt to prepare her for his response. As he spoke, she gently pushed his hand away. Her reaction to his gesture caused him to pause before answering.

"Don't know. Could be trouble."

He had just finished speaking when a stranger's voice came over the CB. "Turn off your lights and stay in the trucks."

Before Chet could reach his mic, Bruce responded.

"Identify yourself!"

The stranger's voice responded with a tone on the edge of anger. "I said turn off your lights and stay in the trucks! Comply and you will not be harmed!"

"CR, CR. Are you getting this?"

Chet already had his finger on the mic button. "Yeah, what do ya think?"

The stranger's voice interrupted the conversation.

"We are approaching you from all sides. Now turn off the lights and step out of the trucks with your hands in the air."

Chet saw the lights of the Expedition go off and the interior light come on as Bruce and Jud got out of the vehicle. He looked at Ruby and the girl in the bunk.

"I'm getting out, but you stay here with her. Stay low and lock the doors."

Chet left the shotgun under the seat and nodded toward it as he climbed down. Ruby saw the gesture and nodded back. She hit the lock button, crawled down onto the floor, and rested her hand on the shotgun stock.

The crunching sounds of boots on gravel approached from ahead. Then the voice that had been on the radio spoke from the darkness.

"Keep your hands up and join your friends."

Chet could see the dim images of Bruce and Jud walking toward him with their hands in the air.

Bruce stopped a few feet ahead of Chet and turned toward the voice. Jud had moved behind Chet and pressed himself against the truck's bumper.

"We are the Redeemers Clan, and we are here to rescue your cargo. If you interfere you will be killed. Do you understand?"

Both Chet and Bruce nodded in agreement and Chet asked a question. "Rescue our cargo? What are you talkin' about?"

"Are you saying you do not know what you are carrying?"

Chet let his hands come down to his side.

"No. The box is locked and sealed."

A tall stout man in his forties wearing a tattered military camouflage jacket and holding a military Ka-Bar knife in his right hand stepped close enough for them to see him.

"You really don't know?"

Before Chet could respond, Ruby suddenly turned on the headlights. In less than one second, while the tall stout man was blinded by the lights, Bruce grabbed the man's right arm, spun him around, and held him from behind as a shield. In the move he had the razor-sharp tip of the knife pressed against the man's neck.

In the beam of light ahead of the truck, they could see a small group of men and women armed with machetes, hatchets, and crossbows.

Bruce called out, "Lay your weapons down and walk this way."

A short heavyset man also wearing a camouflage jacket stepped forward and laid his pistol on the ground. Without speaking, the rest of the group followed his lead. They walked slowly toward the big rig until Bruce spoke up.

"Far enough. Now sit!"

They quickly obeyed, but the heavyset man remained standing.

"Let my lieutenant go."

"Did you say lieutenant?"

"Yes. We are the Redeemers Clan and we mean you no harm. Our mission is to save the young women in that trailer."

Bruce lowered the knife to his side and released his hold on his captor. He could not believe what he was hearing and turned to Chet who was standing next to him with his head slumped forward.

"My God! What have we gotten ourselves into?"

CHAPTER 19

Highway 461 North of Gallup, NM

"Please let me introduce myself. I am Captain Lewis, commander of the Redeemers Clan. I must say I am impressed as you just overpowered my best man, Lieutenant Marks."

The Angels of Light watched and received more orders.

BOND THE CHOSEN TO THE REDEEMERS.
YES, LORD.

As Captain Lewis spoke, the others rose to their feet and moved to stand behind him. The group was a mix of middle-aged men and women, all with faces smeared in black face paint and dressed in tattered desert camouflage clothing.

"We hold and enforce the divine calling and moral duty to save the women being captured and shipped to OHO breeding facilities."

Chet tried to speak, but Captain Lewis held up his hand and continued. "We estimate that camera drones will soon be searching for this truck. Therefore, we cannot delay."

Chet looked up at Ruby, still watching from the cab of the big rig, and wondered how she would react when she learned of their cargo and destination.

Bruce handed Lieutenant Marks the Ka-Bar knife, placed his hand on the lieutenant's shoulder, and asked, "We good?"

When Lieutenant Marks nodded in the affirmative, Bruce turned toward Captain Lewis.

"My name is Bruce Coal, and this is my partner Chet Rawlins. What can we do?"

71

With a hand gesture Captain Lewis signaled to the assembly behind him causing them to separate into two groups. One group disappeared into the darkness and the other moved to the sides of the trailer. Within a few minutes, two battered pickup trucks pulled up and parked on each side of the trailer directly under the red OHO logo and another backed up against the trailer rear doors.

Captain Lewis reached out and shook hands with Bruce and Chet.

"We are glad you are willing to help. We hate killing, but sometimes there is no other way. As for your duties, it is simple. You will continue on to the Gallup Legion Compound with me riding in the truck with you, Mr. Rawlins, and Lieutenant Marks riding with you, Mr. Coal."

When he finished speaking, he walked toward the side of the trailer where the clan members were applying yellow letters over the red OHO logo.

Bruce and Chet followed him, and as they passed the cab, Ruby opened the door.

"What is going on? Who are these people?"

Captain Lewis had seen her through the windshield and assumed she had been the one who flashed on the big rig lights.

"Well, what have we here?"

Bruce answered, "Captain, this is Ruby."

Ruby climbed down from the cab and stood between Chet and Bruce. Chet turned toward her intending to tell her what he had learned about their cargo, but Captain Lewis spoke out first.

"We are running out of time here. I will brief you on our mission on the way to Gallup."

Ruby looked at Chet. "What does he mean 'our mission'?"

Captain Lewis interrupted again. "Please, I will explain everything after we get moving. We are running out of time."

Jud slowly approached them and cleared his throat before speaking. "Uh, maybe I'll just get my stuff and go."

Captain Lewis's response was swift and firm causing Jud to step back. "Absolutely not! You will ride in the escort vehicle with Mr. Coal."

Then he called out to Lieutenant Marks, "Marks! Take this man to the escort vehicle and stay with him."

As Lieutenant Marks and Jud disappeared into the darkness, Captain Lewis turned to Bruce. "What do you know about that man?"

"Actually, sir, we found him along side of the road with a wrecked pickup. Don't really know anything about him. But he had an injured girl with him."

Captain Lewis looked toward the big rig.

"My God! Is she in there as well?"

Chet stepped into the conversation.

"Yes, she's in there, and Ruby is takin' care of her. She has a concussion and hasn't come out of it since we found her."

Captain Lewis ran his left hand over his full white beard contemplating how to handle the new challenge. He turned to Ruby. "Well, this is getting pretty damn complicated. It is my intention to take you with us to protect you from the Enforces at the checkpoint."

The tone of Ruby's voice made her position very clear. "I will not be separated from Bruce and Chet!"

Captain Lewis drew a deep breath as if preparing to render a verdict. "In that case, you and the injured girl must continue on in the trailer."

Ruby looked toward Chet with fear in her eyes and asked, "Is that possible?"

"We won't know till we see what's in there."

Captain Lewis turned and walked toward the rear doors of the box trailer. "Follow me."

Ruby, Bruce, and Chet watched the clan members cut the seals and pick the locks. They worked while standing on the bed of the pickup backed up against the box trailer's rear doors. When the big doors swung open, a rush of cool, antiseptic scented air spilled onto the ground and flowed across their feet.

Captain Lewis and a short matronly gray-haired woman entered the dark void of the trailer with flashlights in hand. They slowly made their way forward, occasionally stopping before moving on. As the flashlight beams moved along the trailer, Ruby, Bruce, and Chet could see shallow bunks stacked three high along both sides of the trailer walls and dozens of small green lights blinking from the foot of the bunks.

Captain Lewis's voice echoed from deep inside the trailer. "Mr. Coal, bring your women in. We have places for them, and hurry."

Chet had carried the unconscious girl from the big rig cab, and with help from Bruce and Ruby, he eased her up on to the pickup truck bed.

Chet could see the look of uncertainty in Ruby's eyes as she spoke, "I'm scared. Can we really trust these people?"

"We can trust them, and you can trust me. I won't let anything happen to you or the girl."

Bruce stooped, picked the girl up, and with a nod of his head, signaled Ruby and Chet to follow him into the dark trailer. Their eyes adjusted to the darkness as they made their way forward, moving slowly toward the light projecting from Captain Lewis and the gray-haired woman's flashlights. As they passed the stacks of bunks, it became obvious that there were young women strapped in place and covered with thin white blankets. The blinking glow of the green lights shown across the blankets providing a hint of female forms laying face up in the bunks they passed.

CHAPTER 20

Legion Compound, Gallup, NM

The first light of morning shone across the town of Gallup, New Mexico, and the Legion Compound.

The compound covered the entire overpass where Highway 491 meets Interstate 40 and several hundred yards of the interstate to the east. The perimeter was secured with concrete barriers and steel gates at the on-and-off ramps, and the remaining open areas were strung with six-foot-high razor wire. To the naked eye, the Enforcer's black uniforms and black helmets with matte-black bulletproof face plates all looked the same. No rank insignia or name tag. No evidence of weapons, cameras, or radio, and except for height and girth, no indication of gender or strength

The Legion commander reviewed the OHO schedule for information about the red trailer coming in from Pagosa Springs. He discovered that it had left Pagosa Springs six hours later than scheduled and ordered the deployment of a camera-drone to fly Highway 491 in search of the truck.

The drone was launched one hour later and began feeding video images back to the Legion Compound. Its mission was to sweep Highway 491 from the compound north to the limit of its range.

At a location thirty miles north, the drone came upon a red tractor with a white trailer followed by a black escort vehicle. It circled and held position at the side of the trailer. It was then that the commander saw the yellow OHO logo. The manifest had called for a red trailer, not yellow.

The commander's voice boomed over the intercom to the desk of his secretary, Lieutenant Omar. "Get in here!"

In mere seconds Lieutenant Omar was standing at attention at the commander's desk.

"Yes, sir."

The commander slowly looked up from his desk and made eye contact with the young lieutenant. "Bring in the drone and man the gate. We have in-bound OHO Yellow."

"Yes, sir."

The commander's stern look and the wave of his hand were followed by grumbled instructions. "Now, get out."

The lieutenant rushed across the open area between the commander's office and the dome structure that housed the thirteen-man troop of Enforcers. He burst through the canvas door. The Enforcer who had been lying on the bunk closest to the door jumped to his feet.

"Jesus…. You scared the crap out of me. What the hell's going on?"

"An OHO Yellow is coming in. Commander says man the gate."

His words got the attention of the other Enforcers. The tallest one marched toward him with his right hand raised and gloved finger pointing at the lieutenant's chest.

"Yellow, my ass! I saw the sheet. It's supposed to be red."

The lieutenant backed toward the door and repeated the instructions as he left. His voice carried no authority or indication of his rank over them. "Just man the gate."

They ignored his order, huddled together, and complained as only disgruntled soldiers can.

"Stinkin' yellow. Can't have no fun with that."

The other Enforcers laughed and gathered their gear.

*****

Chet had seen the drone approach and was watching it in the big outside mirror as it hovered next to the trailer logo, keeping perfect pace with their sixty miles per hour speed.

Captain Lewis spoke from his hiding place in the sleeper. "Tell me when it leaves."

"It just banked away. Looks like its heading back south."

"Good. When you are sure it is out of sight, I want you and the escort vehicle to pull over. We don't have much time."

Chet responded with a word he had used in his days as an airline pilot. "Wilco."

Will comply.

To avoid the risk of having their radio transmission intercepted, he did not call Bruce. Instead he turned on the emergency flashers and slowly pulled over to the shoulder. Bruce understood the covert move and did not use his radio.

Captain Lewis climbed out of the cab and walked briskly back to Bruce's Expedition where he found Lieutenant Marks, Bruce, and Jud standing near the trailer doors.

"Mr. Coal, this is where Lieutenant Marks, Mr. Acres, and I leave you…"

Bruce indicated his understanding by nodding his head in the affirmative.

Jud interrupted. "Wait, what? How am I getting to Gallup?"

Captain Lewis nodded to Lieutenant Marks. "Take him to the rendezvous location."

Jud stepped back and exclaimed. "I'm not walking all the way to Gallup…and I need my stuff."

Captain Lewis raised the authority level of his voice and addressed Lieutenant Marks, as if Jud was not standing there. "We do not have time for this. Get his 'stuff' and get him out of here."

Bruce stepped closer to Captain Lewis, giving him his full attention and waited for him to speak first.

"Mr. Coal, I have advised Mr. Rawlins on the best way to handle the Legion checkpoint. I do not expect them to open the trailer because it is now yellow. However, if they do attempt to cut the seals, you must demand that an officer named Lieutenant Omar grant per mission. Also, as you approach the gate, I want your escort vehicle in the lead…not behind. You will understand as events unfold. That is all the time we have. Use your radio with caution and Godspeed."

He turned and walked away into the desert in the direction that Lieutenant Marks had taken Jud.

Ruby was fast asleep wrapped in several blankets, fending off the cold and not aware that the big rig had stopped.

Bruce walked back to the Expedition and saw Chet watching him in the big side mirror. Chet's arm extended out the window with a thumbs-up signal. Bruce returned the signal and climbed into the Expedition.

CHAPTER 21

Desert Northwest of Gallup, NM

Jud stumbled and dropped to his knees on the rough, sandy ground cursing as he fell. He looked up just in time to see Lieutenant Marks reach down and pull him up by the collar of his shirt.

Lieutenant Marks grumbled his instructions as he pushed Jud forward.

"Trucks up ahead. Get going."

Less than fifty yards ahead stood a line of dust-covered pickup trucks and SUVs partially covered with branches and earth-colored blankets. Lieutenant Marks led Jud to the small pickup truck at the end of the line. His frustration with the assignment of dealing with Jud carried in his actions and voice.

"Get in!"

Jud attempted to resist, but before he could act or speak, Lieutenant Marks grabbed him by the crotch and neck and body-slammed him onto the truck bed. He then turned and gave instructions to a nearby clansman.

"Bag him and ride back here with him."

Without a word spoken, the clansman hopped into the truck bed and pulled a black bag over Jud's head. When Jud tried to pull it off, the clansman grabbed his wrists, pulled Jud's hands behind his back, and zip-tied his wrists together.

The clansman's voice was deep and stern. "Sit in silence and we'll get along. It's a long ride home."

The remaining vehicles were uncovered, loaded up, and the convoy began to roll slowly across the desert floor. Lieutenant Marks drove the lead pickup with two clansmen riding in the bed, each armed with a crossbow.

The SUVs carrying Captain Lewis followed close behind, and the pickup truck with Jud and his guard took up the rear.

As the convoy picked up speed, billows of gritty dust surrounded Jud and his guard, which prompted the guard to pull a respirator over his nose and mouth.

The black bag over Jud's head was his only protection from the dust cloud, and after a few minutes it was worthless. With each breath he took, fine powdery dust migrated through the bag into his nose and mouth, which caused his nose to itch. He had no way to get relief other than craning his neck to the side and trying to rub his nose against his shoulder. That proved to be an almost fatal mistake. Just as he was twisting his neck and bringing his shoulder up to his nose, the pickup bounced through a shallow ditch.

The guard heard the sound of Jud's head slamming against the side of bed and watched him slump to the floor, knocked out cold.

That last bounce brought the convoy onto the semi-smooth pavement of Highway 191 South. Had Jud been conscious and able to see, he may have realized that he was back on the road where the old Indian gave him a ride north, to Klagetoh, Arizona.

The convoy rolled south toward the Redeemers Camp deep in the Sitgreaves National Forest.

CHAPTER 22

Legion Compound, Gallup, NM

They drove in silence with Bruce following the big rig until they crested the last hill before Gallup.

Chet keyed the mic. "BC. Time."

Bruce responded by accelerating around the big rig and took the lead. The mountains south of Gallup, the Interstate Highway, and the Legion Compound surrounding the overpass lay directly ahead. He could not remember the last time he prayed, but as the checkpoint drew near, he found himself asking God for a miracle.

"If You're out there, we sure could use some help about now. God, I hope this works."

Speed limit signs with ever decreasing limits slid past, and within fifty yards of the gate they were crawling along at five miles per hour. Although it was midmorning, several eye-level spotlights came on with such glaring intensity that Bruce lowered his sun visor, like driving into a setting sun. He pulled to a stop several yards from the black iron gate and heard the big rig air brakes hiss behind him.

Bruce waited a few minutes then opened the door and began to step out. Suddenly a booming voice rang out from a public address speaker.

"Remain in the vehicle."

Bruce quickly complied. He looked in the rearview mirrors in an attempt to see Chet, but the truck had stopped so close that only the big radiator was in view.

Then another public address boomed from the speakers.

"Your escort vehicle is in violation of Convey Protocol. Remain in the vehicle. Place all weapons on the dashboard where we can see them."

81

Bruce complied.

"Place your hands on top of your head and do not move."

Again, Bruce complied.

Chet stayed in the cab just as Captain Lewis had instructed, watching and listening as events unfolded.

Five Enforcers came into view from a small structure on the right side of the gate. One stayed in place and four stepped through an opening in the gate, marching in unison toward the Expedition. As they approached, they split into two groups of two stopping a few feet from the drivers and passenger doors.

Bruce's military mind ran various scenarios, and he decided to start with submission and compliance. It was clear that chumming it up with these guys would not work. At least not right away.

His windows were down. With his eyes looking straight ahead and his hands, fingers locked, on top of his head he spoke.

"Sorry about the Convoy Protocol screwup."

The Enforcers were indistinguishable except for size and height. Having no rank insignias or name tags, he could not tell which of them would likely respond. But it was a moot point because they communicated in sequence starting with the Enforcer closest to him.

Enforcer One, "You're not the first to screw it up."

Enforcer Two, "Open the door and step out with your hands where they are."

Enforcer Three, "Move to the front of the vehicle and lay face down over the hood."

Enforcer Four, "You, in the truck. Climb down from the cab and walk backward toward us with your hands on your head."

Enforcer One, "Stop there and do not move."

Enforcers Three and Four moved to each side of Chet and walked him backward to the Expedition where they spun and pushed him against the right front fender. The push forced him against the fender and bent him over with his chest on the hood.

As Enforcer Three and Four walked away to join the others, Bruce and Chet made brief eye contact across the hood. In that fleeting connection, Bruce made it clear that he would handle whatever came next. Bruce and Chet remained bent over the hood of the

Expedition and watched with their peripheral vision as the Enforcers gathered near the cab of the big rig. After a few minutes in a huddle, one of them climbed into the cab while another stood by the opened driver's door. The remaining two walked toward the Expedition.

"Both of you stand up and put your hands behind your backs."

Bruce straightened up and turned toward the approaching Enforcers. His eyes had the cold steel look that Chet has seen before and his voice carried the same message.

"Bullshit! My orders are to guard this convoy. You will stand down!"

His demeanor and the words spoken in the tone of full military authority caught them by surprise and stopped them in their tracks. Even the Enforcer in the big rig stopped rummaging through the cab and looked in Bruce's direction.

The Enforcer at the gate who heard and saw the exchange picked up the public address system microphone.

"Bring them to me."

Immediately Bruce knew who was in charge. He was not sure if he should pull the Lieutenant Omar card yet, so he waited.

Chet walked around the Expedition and joined Bruce. Under his breath he said, "Wow, that stirred 'em up."

Bruce whispered back, "Gotta use what we got."

Bruce and Chet turned and walked toward the gate before the Enforcers were close enough to be considered escorts. Another of the authority tricks Bruce had up his sleeve.

The two Enforcers at the big rig continued rummaging through Chet's personal belongs. When they found the shotgun under the driver's seat, they held it in the air and called out to the Enforcer at the gate.

"Got an unauthorized weapon here!"

The Enforcer at the gate answered, "Place it on the dashboard."

Then with the wave of his hand he ordered them to come to the gate.

CHAPTER 23

Legion Compound, Gallup, NM

The muffled sounds of unfamiliar men's voices alerted Ruby that they were probably at the Legion Compound. She cautiously rolled off the bunk with blankets wrapped around her shoulders and made her way through the darkness to the wall next to the trailer's big rear doors. The eerie feeling of being entombed with stacks of female bodies triggered emotional tremors, which added to the discomfort of her already shivering body. She had to remind herself that the women strapped in the bunks were alive, but in a drug-induced state bordering on comatose.

She had kept herself occupied by checking the young, injured girl's vital signs and so far, she remained stable.

Ruby whispered a little song her grandmother had sung with her when it was bedtime. "Jesus loves me this I know, for the Bible tells me so."

She slid to the floor and wept softly.

*****

The commander pointed at two of the Enforcers and ordered them to bring the truck and escort vehicle into the compound. Chet started to speak, but Bruce nudged his elbow and shook his head. Chet did not like it but hesitantly complied.

The Enforcer at the gate, who was the commander, wore the same black helmet and matte-black face plate as the other Enforcers. He pointed to Bruce and Chet. "You two, come with me."

They followed him across the compound open area toward the commander's prefabricated, green metal office structure.

Chet's discomfort and concern for Ruby in the trailer caused him to disregard Bruce's nonverbal instructions.

"Your people are not gonna move my truck."

The commander stopped, turned to Chet, and flipped up his face plate exposing pale wrinkled skin, small dark eyes, and hairless face and forehead. The vision caused Chet to blink and take a half step back.

"And why is that?" the commander demanded.

Chet looked straight into the man's menacing eyes, reached into his pocket, and pulled out small black plastic fob.

"Two reasons. One, that's my truck. Two, it won't start without this."

He dangled the fob before the commander and continued. "I'm movin' the truck to wherever you want it. AND I'm stayin' with the truck until it's time to roll the hell outta here."

The commander pulled his face plate down and spoke into the helmet. Neither Bruce nor Chet could hear his words, only the disgruntled mumbling. He pulled his face plate back up and looked at both men.

"Go back to your damn truck. You will be shown where to park it."

Then he turned to Bruce. "You come with me and explain why the schedule shows a red load when you show up with yellow.

Chet rushed back to his truck, and Bruce walked with the commander to the office.

A lone Enforcer was sitting in the passenger's seat with Chet's map case on his lap when Chet opened the driver's door.

"Get outta my truck."

The Enforcer flipped up his face mask, turned, and glared at Chet. His squinting dark eyes were shrouded by bushy, black eyebrows and black beard stubble covered most of his exposed face.

"Not happening. My orders are to stay with the truck and shadow your every move. Got it?"

Chet reached across the cab and pulled the map case from his lap.

"Hang around all you want, but stay outta my stuff."

"Too late for that," he said with a crooked smile. "We're wondering why a trucker would have a Continental Airline map case. You steal it?"

The urgency to check on Ruby prompted him to take a deep breath and speak in a less aggressive tone.

"Yeah, I used to fly, but I can't get into it right now. I need to make sure the reefer is workin'. Last thing we need is a spoiled load."

And with those words he turned and climbed down from the cab. The Enforcer knocked the map case onto the cab floor and called out to Chet as he walked away.

"Yeah, that's another thing we're wondering. This is supposed to be a red load. We may have to open it up and see what the hell's going on."

Chet ignored the threat and climbed up onto the trailer where a small ladder ascended to the refrigeration unit. The unit was mounted high on the trailer's headwall with louvered air vents on each side. As the Enforcer watched from the ground, Chet leaned close to the furthest vent and whispered.

"Ruby, can you hear me?"

Silence.

He waited a few more seconds then tried again, raising his voice slightly.

"Ruby, Ruby."

Ruby thought she heard a voice coming from the front of the trailer calling her name. She crept forward and listened intently.

Chet could not risk raising his voice without being heard by the Enforcer on the ground. The only way to make it work was to distract him.

"Hey. A little help up here."

The Enforcer looked up with his face mask still open and asked, "What?"

Chet nodded toward the cab.

"There is a long, yellow-handled, common screwdriver in a black toolbox under the passenger's seat. I need it."

"What am I, your grunt? Get it yourself."

Chet turned on the ladder and stood facing him with his left arm wrapped around the top rung.

"Look, pal, the reefer is overheating, and I need to get the cover off ASAP. Or should I tell your commander that you caused the load to spoil? Your call."

The Enforcer mumbled something under his breath, turned, and walked to the cab of the tractor.

As soon as the Enforcer's back was turned Chet leaned so close to the vent that his lips brushed against the louvers as he spoke.

"Ruby, are you there? This is Chet. Talk to me."

"Oh god. Chet, what's happening?"

The faint sound of her voice filled him with long-forgotten emotions and tears began to flow. Tears he had not tasted since his mother's death. He took a breath and swallowed hard.

"We're okay out here. Don't know how much longer this will take. Can you make it?"

"Oh, Chet, I'm so afraid."

Chet heard the Enforcer approaching.

"Be strong and quiet. Trust me. We will make it outta here. Hold on."

He climbed down the ladder far enough to reach down and take the screwdriver from the Enforcer's outstretched hand then climbed back up to the reefer. There was no other communication between Chet and the Enforcer other than looks that could kill.

As he pretended to work on the refrigeration unit, he whispered to Ruby. "Are you too cold in there?"

"A little, but I found more blankets and some medical supplies."

"Do you want me to warm it up a little? I can."

Although she craved warmth, she did not know how a temperature change might affect the comatose girls.

"No, we better leave it as it is. I will be okay. Just please get us out of this place."

"We're workin' on it. I will tell you as soon as I know something."

Chet climbed down and slipped into the cab, behind the wheel. The map case was lying on its side with maps and charting tools spilled out onto the cab floor. As Chet gathered up his clothes, blankets, and tools that had been strewn about the cab by the Enforcers, he noticed the case. He reached down and slid the maps, pencils, chart plotter, and hand calculator back into the case and set it on the passenger's seat. One of the maps was wedged between the case hinges with its corner sticking straight up. Chet froze and gasped as his eyes focused on the lines and numbers running along the outside borders.

"Latitude…longitude!"

He pulled out his phone and played the message from Tom he had saved in the phone's memory.

"This is Tom. Don't know where you are, but this will be my last chance to reach you. Remember, God loves you. When things get strange and people disappear, stand under the hope of the promise. Col at Vai three five dot three plus three nine plus six. Then one zero six, dot, three six plus three five plus nine. Under the cross down. God bless and guide you."

He whispered the words.

"Three five, dot…thirty-five degrees."

He paused as the simple reality of the number's portion of the riddle fell into place.

"Three, plus thirty-nine, plus six…three minutes, thirty-nine point six seconds."

He reached into the map case, pulled out a pen and paper, and scribbled frantically before the revelation was lost.

35 degrees, 3 minutes, 39.6 seconds. 106 degrees, 36 minutes, 35.9 seconds.

He reached back into the map case and pulled out a map of North America. Gliding the tip of the pen along the map, he found the latitude and longitude intersection described in the riddle.

Albuquerque, New Mexico. Just southwest of the International Airport.

Chapter 24

Legion Compound, Gallup, NM

The commander's office was cool and stark. Bruce sat in a gray steel chair in front of the commander's steel desk and waited. He watched as the man removed his helmet and gloves exposing his totally bald scalp and skin as pale and wrinkled as his face. He moved slowly to the desk, sat down, and slid a one-page document across the uncluttered desktop toward Bruce. In a relaxed almost friendly tone he asked, "Military?"

Bruce understood the question and answered respectfully, "Marine, just retired."

"Thought you might be. You took a risk out there telling my men to stand down. That took some balls."

Bruce nodded and shifted in his chair, leaning slightly closer. "Improvise. It kept me alive in some worse spots than that, sir. I just had to wait until I knew who was in charge."

The commander's face remained emotionless, but Bruce sensed by the tone of his voice and body language that mutual respect could be developing.

"Sir, I can't explain the paperwork SNAFU, but I do know this…we got a late start and we really need to make up some time on the interstate."

The commander chuckled. "SNAFU…Situation Normal, All F'd Up. Haven't heard that one in years."

He leaned forward and placed his pale hands on the desktop with his fingers entwined. His facial expression became somber and judgmental.

"Do you know the difference between Red and Yellow loads?"

Bruce did not respond.

The commander leaned back and continued as if lecturing a room of students.

"Yellow trailers carry near frozen human bodies and various organs harvested from suicides. Dissidents and those who hamper the establishment of order are captured and beheaded. It has been proven that beheading is the most humane and beneficial method of execution. You see, in a beheading there is no damage to tissue or organs and no blood-borne pathogens. As such, your yellow trailer is critical for research and the saving of worthy lives. We consider it 'death for the benefit of life.'"

The reality of what was happening in the world outside hit Bruce like a punch in the chest. He struggled to maintain composure as the commander continued.

"The red trailers have a different and extremely important role in the survival of humanity. We consider it 'life for the benefit of the future.'"

Bruce knew what the red trailers hauled and waited to hear the commander's spin on the atrocity.

"We do not yet know why or how the planet was rid of one-third of the adult population and all children less than thirteen years of age. Although religious conspiracy theories abound, scientists believe the event was a massive alien abduction. Unfortunately, their investigation is hampered by the loss of all space-borne equipment, which may in fact have been part of the alien invasion plan."

He briefly looked down at his desk, tapped his index finger on a document in front of Bruce, and continued.

"Breeders. Young women of child-bearing quality. That is humanity's only hope for survival. Without them, mankind will slip into oblivion." He picked up the document, tossed it into a round metal waste basket next to his deck, and abruptly stood up. The move caught Bruce by surprise. He withheld the instinct to stand and take a defensive posture. The commander turned and looked out the window.

"I am ordering an inspection of the trailer."

Bruce began to speak but was cut off by the commander shouting into the intercom on his desk.

"Lieutenant Omar! Get in here!"

Just as suddenly, the commander's office was pierced by Lieutenant Omar's voice.

"Sir."

The commander was standing at the window looking across the compound at the yellow trailer. Bruce was standing near the door when the lieutenant entered the office.

The commander turned abruptly and barked an order, "Bring me the cargo master key and yellow tags."

The lieutenant glanced at Bruce then turned to the commander.

"Sir, I am sorry, but we do not have any yellow tags."

"What! You were ordered to requisition tags weeks ago. This is unacceptable, Lieutenant."

"I am sorry, sir, but delays at headquarters have effected every requisition I have sent in."

The commander lowered his head and glared at the floor.

"And sir, we have a group of representatives from Capitia arriving tomorrow morning. I am concerned that it is an evaluation inspection."

"Damn it, Lieutenant, when were you planning to tell me about that? Don't answer that! Leave us!"

The commander waited until the door had closed and turned to Bruce with a look of suspicion on his face.

"I don't like this one damn bit, Coal. However, I cannot risk my career over a, what did you call it…SNAFU? I want you and that damn truck off my compound."

He stomped to his desk and smashed a key on the intercom.

"Get departure forms and fuel cards for the vehicles and escort Mr. Coal out of here. I want that convoy off my compound."

He had barely removed his hand from the intercom when Lieutenant Omar came through the door with a large white envelope clutched in his left hand.

"Follow me, Mr. Coal."

During their walk across the compound, Bruce whispered, "So, you are the Lieutenant Omar I was told could help."

The lieutenant spoke while looking straight ahead, "Just doing my job."

As they neared the Expedition, he handed Bruce the white envelope. It was similar to the envelope they received in Pagosa Springs. The difference was the large yellow OHO stamp.

"Fuel depot is ahead at the Westbound on-ramp. Godspeed."

He turned, walked away, and never looked back.

Chet rushed over.

"What's up?"

Bruce smiled and patted the envelope.

"We're outta here."

CHAPTER 25

Legion Compound, Gallup, NM

The growl and rumble of the big diesel engine and the lurch of forward motion woke Ruby from a self-induced trancelike state. She had been locked in the trailer for over six hours. Chet's words, playing over and over in her mind, had helped her maintain composure. *Be strong and quiet...trust me.* She felt new hope rising in her heart.

At first, she thought the brush of something against on her arm was from the rocking movement of the trailer as it gained speed, then she heard a moan. She turned toward the bunk of the young unconscious girl and gently placed her right hand over her eyes, brushed her cheek, and knelt down with her ear close to the girl's nostrils. No fever and very shallow breathing. The trailer abruptly slowed down causing Ruby to grasp the bunk frame with her left hand to steady herself.

Another moan was followed by the soft flutter of the girl's eyelashes against Ruby's palm. A quick check of heart rate and respiration confirmed that she could awaken at any moment. The last thing Ruby wanted was to have her come to in the horror of the dark trailer. During the hours inside the trailer, she had rummaged through every storage box and cabinet looking for medical supplies. She pulled a package of tranquilizer pills from her pocket and quickly slipped two pills between the girl's lips and under her tongue.

Ruby prayed.

"God, please make this work."

Within minutes the girl's heart rate and respiration slowed.

Ruby felt the truck slow to a stop. Almost immediately she heard the sound of someone climbing the trailer head-wall followed by Chet's voice through the vent.

"Ruby, you awake?"

"Yes. What is happening?'

"We're fuelin' up and getting' outta here. Should have you out of there in a couple hours."

The joy of escape was quickly overshadowed by the reality of two more hours locked up in the cold trailer. The disappointment carried in her voice.

"Two more hours?"

"Yeah. We can't open the trailer till we get somewhere safe."

"Chet…is Bruce with us?"

"Yeah, he is gassin' up the Expedition. We'll be rollin' in a few minutes. Hang on."

Chet climbed down the ladder and did not hear her sad reply.

"Okay."

PART THREE
Amalgamation

CHAPTER 26

Truck Stop, Winslow, AZ

Winslow, Arizona, had been a small struggling community before The Vanishing took its toll. Now all it had to offer was fuel and vehicle repair at a truck stop off Interstate 40, one hundred and twenty-five miles west of Gallup.

They had been rolling for almost two hours, and the off-ramp for Winslow was just over the next rise.

Chet keyed the mic. "BC, BC."

"Go."

Both men were relieved and grateful for having escaped the Legion Compound, and both were anxious to get Ruby out of the trailer.

"How we doin' back there?"

Bruce understood the coded question.

"Flying solo, looking for a break."

Chet sighed in relief. *Flying solo…*the drone that had been tracking them since leaving Gallup was gone. *Looking for a break…* stop and get the girls out.

Bruce did not know that Captain Lewis had instructed Chet to meet a contact at the Winslow truck stop where they would be given the next step in the plan to free the captives.

Chet radioed Bruce.

"Exit comin' up in a couple miles. Follow me in."

"You know I will."

The only traffic they had encountered since leaving Gallup had been slow moving military convoys and an eastbound gray passenger bus with the windows blacked out.

There was no other traffic in sight when Chet slowed and merged onto the off-ramp at Trans-con Lane. At the stop sign at the bottom of the ramp, he turned left under the freeway and left again at the truck stop entrance. Chet pulled into the diesel lane set up for big rigs, and Bruce stopped at the gasoline pumps closer to the entrance of the building.

A tall thin middle-aged man dressed in a brown mechanics jumpsuit and wearing a red baseball cap was leaning on the wall near the building entrance. He watched casually as they pulled in. Chet climbed down from the cab and walked to the building entrance. When he reached the door, the man in the red cap nodded and opened the door for him.

"You Rawlins?'

Chet was caught off guard by the question and looked around before answering.

"I am. Who's askin?"

"Me and Captain Lewis. Get your fuel ordered and meet me behind the building near the dumpsters. He nodded toward the Expedition.

"Bring him with you."

*****

Chet paced back and forth along the wall between the dumpster and rear of the truck stop. The stench coming from the dumpster was only tolerable due to the brisk west wind whipping around the corner of the building. Bruce leaned on the upwind wall.

The man in the red cap appeared through a rear door marked Employees Only. He walked over to Bruce and signaled Chet to join them.

"We move at eight o'clock."

He nodded toward a row of vehicles parked along the rear wall of the building.

"Watch for the red pickup and follow it. I want the Expedition behind me and the tractor trailer taking up the rear."

He stepped back and turned toward Chet.

"Between now and then I suggest you move your personal belongings to the Expedition."

He disappeared through the "Employees Only" door before Chet could ask why.

The sun was close to the horizon signifying that they would be moving out in less than an hour. The urgency to check on Ruby and tell her what was transpiring competed with Chet's suspicion that he may lose his truck.

CHAPTER 27

Redeemers Clan, AZ

Before the Redeemers Clan took over, the grassy meadow and winding creek that flowed along the base of a red-rock cliff face had been known as Chevelon Creek Campgrounds.

It was perfect in its seclusion, resources, and for controlling access by road. The steep, rocky, one-lane road from the south winds down into Chevelon Canyon before reaching the narrow concrete bridge over the creek at the meadow. The steep grade and twisting turns caused approaching traffic to slow to a crawl, which gives the lookouts ample time to alert the camp.

After passing over the bridge and through the meadow, the road winds up the opposite side of the canyon and continues north to Winslow, Arizona. It was along the 125-mile stretch between the Redeemers' camp and Winslow that the Redeemers had laid a telegraph cable from the camp's north lookout blind to an old barn on the south side of Winslow.

The first shadows of evening floated across the Redeemers' camp as Lieutenant Marks approached Captain Lewis's tent. As was his habit of confirming situation awareness, he glanced left and right before stopping at the tent threshold. The camp was quiet and void of activity except for the sounds of nurses talking in the nearby hospital tent. He tapped on the wooden tent post and waited.

Captain Lewis's response was quick and authoritative. "Yes!"

"Lieutenant Marks, sir. May I have a moment?"

The sound of a chair sliding on the wood floor preceded Captain Lewis's answer. "Enter."

Lieutenant Marks slipped through the tent flap with Jud's backpack hanging from his forearm. He stopped just inside the threshold and waited for permission to approach. The wood floor reflected a polished sheen as did the wooden slab of Captain Lewis's desk. His bunk was on the left and his wardrobe on the right. Lieutenant Marks knew that if he was to toss a coin onto the dark brown wool blanket stretched over the bunk it would bounce as if on a trampoline.

Captain Lewis sat down behind his desk and gestured toward the folding chair across from him. "Sit. What do you have there?"

"It is the pack the new man Jud brought with him."

"I do recall. Why are you bringing it to me?"

Lieutenant Marks placed the backpack onto his lap, slipped his hand inside, and pulled a small Bible. The black leather cover and gold-embossed letters looked as new. He first held it out for Captain Lewis to see and set it on the desk.

"Interesting. Do you have an idea of why he would have that?"

"I do, sir. I found it when I inspected the backpack and asked how he got it. His answer was revealing."

Captain Lewis leaned forward and placed his hands on the desk. "What did he reveal?

"He said it didn't matter how he got it. What mattered was how much it was worth to me."

"He wants to barter, does he? So be it. Leave it here with me and return the backpack to him. To what duties have you assigned him?"

"Kitchen crew and pathway maintenance."

Captain Lewis stood and walked around the desk to face Lieutenant Marks.

"See if he is qualified to man one of the lookouts."

"Sir, that requires Morse code."

The two men walked toward the tent threshold.

"I am aware of that. Consider it a test and watch him closely."

"Good night, sir."

"Good night, Lieutenant."

As the tent flap fell closed, Captain Lewis walked back to his desk, picked up the Bible, and whispered.

"Thank you, Lord. I see the confirmation and now I know they are the ones."

What Captain Lewis and Lieutenant Marks did not know was that Jud had hidden the little red Bible inside the backpack padding.

CHAPTER 28

Redeemers Clan, AZ

Jud was alone in the north lookout blind where he not only had a clear view of the road but also an unobstructed view of the women's compound in the meadow below. He used binoculars as a voyeur to scan the meadow and creek hoping to see some exposed female flesh. To his gratification, he spotted a group of young girls standing knee deep in the water along the shore bending over, dipping and pulling freshly washed clothes from the flow. Their gray cotton gowns clung to their bodies as they playfully splashed each other while they worked.

He was totally focused on the wet girls when the Morse code receiver suddenly buzzed indicating that a message would be coming in the next few minutes. The loud audible interruption shocked him out of the lustful fantasy and caused him to bang his head on a log beam overhead.

He had hoped no messages would come in primarily because he had lied about knowing Morse code when Lieutenant Marks assigned him to lookout duty. He was also sure he could probably fake it if it happened.

In the process of reaching up to rub the knot forming on the back of his head, he dropped the binoculars sending them crashing onto the dirt floor.

He grabbed up the binoculars and was attempting to wipe off the grit and dirt when the buzzer sounded again followed by the long and short tapping of a Morse coded message.

The sound of a vehicle climbing up the road from the camp caught his attention prompting him to grab a pencil and notebook lying on the shelf next to the receiver. He scribbled a few nonsensical phrases and waited.

A black, dust-covered pickup truck stopped and Lieutenant Marks stepped out. As he slammed the door shut, a fist-sized piece of dried mud fell from the rear wheel well.

Jud turned toward him as he entered the blind.

"We got a message…but missed it."

Lieutenant Marks looked over Jud's shoulder and attempted to read the scribbling on the notebook.

"What in the hell is this?"

"Like I said, I missed it."

Lieutenant Marks pushed him away from the receiver, pulled a canvas folding camp chair up to the receiver shelf, and sat down.

"How long ago?"

"How long ago, what?"

Lieutenant Marks's loathing of Jud came through in his words and tone of voice.

"The message, dumbass. Did it just come in?"

Jud frowned at the name-calling and growled the answer. "Yeah, it just came in…asshole."

Lieutenant Marks ignored the remark and tapped out a quick message. "Repeat, repeat."

Within a few seconds he received a response. "Trailer here. Advise."

Lieutenant Marks tapped out the needed instruction. "Meet us at 2100 hours."

"Clear."

After the last message, the man in the red cap covered the equipment, locked up the old barn, and rode his bicycle back to the truck stop.

CHAPTER 29

Southwest of Winslow, AZ

The eight-vehicle convoy of six SUVs and two pickup trucks rumbled north across the dark open plains throwing gravel and dust into the air. Dried mud and layers of dust covering the vehicles created a natural camouflage, and the slotted covers over the headlights helped reduce detection at night. The rear seats of the SUVs had been removed to accommodate long payloads, and metal rings were bolted to the floor for attachment of tie-down straps that were coiled up and scattered around the ribbed rubber floor.

They were heading for a truck graveyard located one mile southwest of the Winslow airport. The same trip, for the same reason, had been successful twice before, but there were no guarantees. Timing and efficiency were paramount.

At the exact same moment, Bruce and Chet were following the clansman in the red pickup truck west on Interstate 40. They slowed and exited at Hipkoe Drive then took old Route 66 west for less than a mile. At a narrow, paved road they turned south, crossed over railroad tracks and continued along the dirt road beyond the tracks, passing abandoned homes and outbuildings. They stopped briefly to disconnect the trailer lights and continued on. The only other evidence of activity was the flashing white and green beacon of Winslow airport to the east.

The headlights of Chet's big rig were off, but the low mounted fog lights illuminated the clouds of dust coming from Bruce's Expedition ahead and a six-foot high chain-link fence running parallel with the road. The red pickup slowed and turned through an opening in the chain-link fence. As Chet made the wide turn nec-

105

essary to thread the fifty-three-foot trailer through the opening, his lights swept across the battered remains of big rig tractors and trailers. He mumbled aloud, "Damn it! A graveyard!"

The clansman stopped and waived a flashlight toward a nearby metal building with rows of loading bays. Chet pulled up next to the red pickup and rolled down his window. The clansman stepped out of the pickup and walked over to the big rig. He aimed the flashlight at the loading bays as he spoke.

"Need you to turn off all your lights and back into one of those bays. I'll guide you."

Bruce joined them and offered to help guide the trailer through the dark graveyard.

Meanwhile, inside the trailer, six of the twenty blinking green lights had changed to red. Ruby was lying unconscious on the trailer floor unaware of the tragic loss of six lives, plus one.

*****

The battery-powered walkie-talkie in Captain Lewis's right hand was purposefully limited to a maximum range of two hundred yards. As the convoy slowed and stopped on the dirt road near the truck graveyard, he pressed the transmit button.

"Red Cap, Red Cap."

The response was quick.

"Red here and ready."

Captain Lewis raised his left hand and pointed ahead as he concluded the communication with Red Cap.

"Inbound five out."

Lieutenant Marks obeyed the nonverbal instructions, and the convoy continued through the darkness toward the opening in the chain-link fence.

Meanwhile Chet and Bruce stood by the trailer doors impatiently waiting for the clansman called Red Cap to cut the lock.

Bruce rested his right hand on Chet's shoulder and spoke softly, "Almost there, buddy. Almost there."

Chet nodded but kept his eyes fixed on the doors. He had called out to Ruby through the vents, and when she did not answer he knew that something was wrong. Suddenly, with a loud pop, like a firecracker exploding, the bolt cutter sliced through the lock. Chet rushed forward pushing Red Cap aside with his shoulder and pulled the doors open. A surge of cold putrid air and horrible silence poured out from the darkness.

Red Cap grabbed Chet's right arm in an attempt to hold him back.

"Stop! You can't go in there till Captain Lewis gets here."

He ignored the warning and tried to pull away from the man's grip. Bruce stepped between the two men, grabbed Red Cap's wrist, and twisted. Red Cap dropped to his knees and groaned.

"Damn it, you can't go in there."

Bruce held Red Cap in place and handed Chet a flashlight.

"Go, I've got this."

The stench of urine, feces, and death that hung in the air caused Chet to hold his hand over his mouth and nose to keep form gagging.

He shouted out as he crept forward through the darkness.

"Ruby! I'm here!"

Deadly silence.

The flashlight beam waved past bunks, some with blinking green lights and others red. As he neared the front of the trailer, the flashlight beam swept across a lump of blankets on the floor. He knelt down and gently pulled them away. It was Ruby. His voice echoed as he called out to Bruce.

"She's passed out!"

Chet slid his arms under her shoulders and legs and lifted her as he stood. The blankets fell away onto the damp floor. He turned toward the trailer doors and called out, "We're comin' out."

Captain Lewis stood alone in the trailer door opening with his arms crossed over his chest watching Chet approach with Ruby in his arms.

CHAPTER 30

Southwest of Winslow, AZ

Clansmen and clanswomen swarmed over the truck and trailer each with specific duties and time limits. The only evidence of their presence was small beams of light emitting from LED lamps strapped to their foreheads. The two pickup trucks of the convoy had parked at the sides of the trailer and clansmen removed the yellow OHO logos. Then acid wash was sprayed over the underlying red logos, destroying them completely.

Meanwhile, the clan's doctor and head nurse were preparing the fourteen girls who had survived for transport. They were moved from the trailer still unconscious and strapped into their bunks. Each bunk was carefully tied down in the backs of the waiting SUVs. The bodies of those who did not survive were wrapped in white sheets and placed in the bed of Captain Lewis's pickup truck.

Captain Lewis guided Chet, with Ruby in his arms, to the lead SUV where he laid Ruby on a small cot on the ground next to the vehicle's rear hatch. The captain assured Chet that she was in good hands as a young nurse knelt over and checked her vital signs. She looked up at the captain and smiled.

"Her vitals look okay, sir. May I get her out of these soiled clothes?"

"Do it and get her into the vehicle quickly. We leave in fifteen minutes."

He turned to Chet and Bruce who stood at the foot of the cot not knowing how to fit into the mission. In their mutual concern for Ruby, they had completely forgotten the unconscious girl.

Captain Lewis pointed in the direction of the white trailer as he spoke.

"You men, come with me."

They followed him to Chet's big rig and stopped where the tractor connected to the trailer.

"Disconnect the trailer and move the tractor to the fuel dump. Red Cap will show you where it is after the trailer is off."

He turned and walked away into the darkness.

Chet sat on the edge of the saddle tank and looked up at Bruce. "I don't like this."

"Me neither, but we don't have much choice right now. Let's get the trailer off so we can get the hell outta here."

As they cranked down the trailer's landing legs and released the fifth wheel, the last of the dead bodies was carried from the trailer.

When Chet climbed into the cab, he noticed that the interior was gutted and banged on the steering wheel as he shouted, "Shit."

Bruce was standing on the driver's side ready to watch the trailer disconnect and heard the shout.

"What!"

"My truck's gutted. Radios gone...bunk stripped...shit!"

The clansman called Red Cap approached the truck and waved his flashlight at the men.

"Follow me...slow like."

Bruce walked toward him at front of the truck and Red Cap stepped back cautiously. Bruce held both hands up with palms facing the man.

"Nothin' to worry about. What's goin' on?"

"Gotta off-load the fuel and mothball the tractor. We're running out of time."

Bruce was familiar with the military term "mothballed" and climbed up to the cab's open window.

"They're gonna mothball it...store it. Sounds like you aren't losing your truck after all."

Chet's only response was to start the truck's engine and lurch forward releasing the trailer and throwing Bruce onto the ground.

*****

Seven female bodies that had been wrapped in white sheets were gently loaded into the back of Captain Lewis's pickup truck. The unconscious girl Ruby had attended was among the deceased. The Redeemers Clan's SUVs followed carrying fourteen unconscious survivors and Ruby. She had not awakened from the accidental overdose of tranquilizers and was not aware that the unconscious girl was dead, also from an overdose.

Bruce and Chet rode alone in silence in the Expedition at the rear of the convoy. A second pickup truck, loaded down with fuel cans and the booty taken from Chet's truck, followed.

As they approached a remote dirt road intersection twenty miles south of Winslow, the lead pickup carrying the bodies slowed and stopped. Captain Lewis, who was riding in the pickup truck, stepped out and with a wave of his arm instructed the convoy to continue on. It was his solemn duty to inter the bodies at a location where no animal or person would disturb the graves. He stood and watched the convoy disappear into the dim light of early morning. Clutched in his right hand was his worn, dark brown leather-covered Bible.

CHAPTER 31

En Route to Redeemers Clan, AZ

Emotional and spiritual dead weight.

If it could speak it would moan. If it could move it would crawl. If it could see it would weep. If it could hear it would argue. If it could attack it would pummel.

Such was the condition of Chet's heart and mind as he and Bruce drove in silence behind the convoy as it headed back to the Redeemers' camp deep in the Sitgreaves National Forest. People he cared for had died or disappeared, and Ruby may not live because he had agreed to lock her in the trailer. His career as an airline pilot had been lost because he withheld and destroyed the Pilot's Log Book of his best friend Tom Winslow. Saving Tom from having his flying career destroyed over an accidental plane crash had in fact destroyed Chet's flying career, but the sacrifice had been worth it.

He had ignored Tom's many pleadings to get right with God, and now Tom and David had vanished and he was still here. His life of relative isolation as a trucker had ended at the truck graveyard where he had thrown Bruce onto the ground and damn near drove over him. He sighed deeply and watched in silence as the passing landscape changed from rolling hills and pinyon pines to canyons, red rock outcroppings, and tall pine trees.

Bruce's military life and the loss of fellow marines in battle gave him compassion for Chet and the burden he carried. He looked briefly toward Chet and knew they would connect again, and when they did, their bond would be stronger. Little did he know that empowering their bond was God's plan.

The convoy slowed as the dirt road twisted down the winding grade to the Redeemers' camp below. A lone clansman stood by the road at the top of the grade waving to the vehicles as they passed.

CHAPTER 32

Truck Stop, Winslow, AZ

A lone motorcycle with an Enforcer in full gear pulled up to the gas pumps at the Winslow truck stop. He dismounted the matte-black motorcycle and waved a Legion Fuel Card across the pump's card reader. His movements were slow and deliberate as he twisted off the fuel cap, inserted the nozzle, and waited. Within minutes a voice came over the intercom at the pump.

"After fueling, please report to the cashier."

He finished fueling the bike and rode the short distance from the pumps to the front of the building. Red Cap was leaning on the wall near the door watching him approach. Enforcers are ordered to never raise their facemasks when off-base. However, as he neared the door, he flipped it up and quickly pulled it back down. The brief exposure of his face was confirmation for Red Cap to open the door and prepare to receive a message. As he walked slowly through the door's opening, a folded piece of paper secretly passed from the Enforcer's gloved hand into Red Cap's waiting palm. The Enforcer made his way on to the cashier's window and Red Cap hopped on his bicycle and rode to the old barn.

After confirming the fuel purchase with the cashier, he moved to the café and found a seat at a booth facing the door with his back to the wall. The tall windows were coated with dust and grim, but the view of the fuel yard and road was sufficient. He pressed the menu button on the table's touch screen surface and ordered a vegan burger, rice, and bottled water. The face masks of Enforcer's helmets were deigned to open sufficiently to allow eating and drinking without exposing nose or eyes. In that mode the voice masking mechanism was disabled. He sat in silence and waited for Red Cap to return.

Before he had finished eating, he saw Red Cap ride into the truck stop. The nod of Red Cap's head as he pedaled past the café windows instructed the Enforcer to come to the back of the building.

After waving his Currency Card over the tabletop payment icon, he lowered his facemask and slowly walked to his waiting motorcycle. The short ride to the rear of the building was interrupted when a young mechanic dressed in a grease-stained jumpsuit flagged him down.

"Need you to walk the rest of the way. Your bike and helmet's going to the shop with me."

The Enforcer flipped up his facemask and glared at him.

"On whose authority?"

A smile crept across the young mechanic's face exposing yellow crooked teeth.

"Me and Captain Lewis."

CHAPTER 33

Legion Compound, Gallup, NM

The Legion commander in Gallup was in his office preparing for the second meeting of the day with the six-person group of Capitia Overseers that had arrived the night before. He fumbled through a loose stack of shipping manifests in a hapless attempt to deflect blame for the two red trailers that had not arrived at the Phoenix, Arizona, OHO Breeding Center.

The ominous gray passenger bus that brought the Overseers was parked outside the commander's office. Three men and three women, dressed in white jumpsuits with white boots and white turban-like head coverings, exited the bus and walked single file toward his office.

He saw them through the window and scrambled to organize the desktop chaos. Lieutenant Omar was nowhere to be found, and the commander intended to have him punished to the fullest extent of Legion Law for abandoning his post at such a crucial time. He mused at the thought for a moment before the door slowly swung open followed by a woman's voice dripping with indignant sarcasm.

"Commander...pardon us for letting ourselves in...again. It appears that you remain...unstaffed."

Anything he could say would make matters worse if that were possible. He stood at attention behind his desk while the group sat down in the chairs he had brought in for the previous morning meeting. His career and possibly his life depended on the outcome of the meeting, and the burden of that fact demoralized him. He sat and submissively placed his hands, fingers entwined, on the desk and did not speak.

It was clear that she was the spokesperson for the group, although on occasion she looked toward the other five who all nodded in unison.

"Commander, as we discussed this morning, we are aware that Legion Enforcers are well trained, disciplined, and loyal to One World Order and Operation Humanity One. However, as I am sure you know, not all are capable of controlling themselves. Hence, it is critical that there be a strong authority controlling them. You, Commander, were to have been that authority."

The words "were to have been" sent cold chills through his body, like hearing one's death sentence proclaimed.

She continued. "Do you have the documentation that you allege exists regarding the two yellow trailers that we believe are in fact the missing red trailers?"

He fumbled through the papers on his desk in an attempt to stall for time to think of an answer.

She reached over and rapped her knuckles on the desktop. "Apparently not."

He began to answer but she interrupted.

"Another equally important problem has come to our attention. We at OHO are aware that red trailers have been opened and the cargo sexually compromised prior to arrival at the Breeding Center. As such, we will be collecting DNA samples from everyone on base, including you, Commander."

Beads of perspiration formed on his hairless scalp and dribbled down his wrinkled face and neck. In an effort to hide his guilt and fear, he leaned back in his chair and folded his arms across his chest. His voice rattled slightly as he spoke. "Madam, I assure you that such an atrocity has not and will not happen on my base or on my watch."

"We will see, Commander... We will see."

They rose in unison and slowly departed the room in single file. When the door finally closed behind them, he fell face down on the desk and released a pathetic moan. Without sitting up, he reached over to the top right desk drawer and pulled out a nine-millimeter pistol. He slid the pistol across the desktop, pushed the barrel against his temple, and pulled the trigger.

The Overseers ignored the gunshot as if it was expected and continued walking to the bus.

CHAPTER 34

Truck Stop, Winslow, AZ

The tall four-bay repair shop reeked of spent oil and diesel exhaust even though the full height overhead doors stood fully opened.

In a remote corner, near the shop supervisor's office, the Enforcer and Red Cap watched a young mechanic approach. Red Cap rested his hand on the Enforcer's shoulder and spoke first.

"Jerry, this is Lieutenant Omar. Omar, Jerry."

Omar nodded, removed his gloves, and held his right hand out in greeting. The flow and tone of his words matched his Middle Eastern appearance.

Omar looked at Red Cap then turned toward Jerry and said, "He tells me you're a whiz with all things electronic."

Jerry wiped his palm on the leg of his jumpsuit, grasped Omar's hand, and gave it a good shake.

"So, you bailed on Legion," he said with a smile that exposed his yellow, crocked teeth. "Pretty cool."

"Not cool if I get caught. Tell me what you did to make sure I don't."

Jerry smiled, reached over, and picked up the matte-black helmet resting on a nearby shelf.

"The tracking devices are ready to be disabled."

He held the helmet up in his left hand and pointed at a red wire extending from under the neck padding.

"All you do is pull this wire all the way out and the tracking is killed. Everything else still works. Radio, voice masking, rearview imaging, weapons selection, heat and cooling, and the re-breather."

Omar looked skeptically at Jerry who then smiled and returned the matte-black helmet.

"Go ahead. Try it. I checked it out myself if you don't believe me."

"No, I believe you. I'm just surprised you can do this."

Jerry sat the helmet on the ground next to the motorcycle.

"Don't let my good looks fool you. I know bikes, I know electronics, and I know Captain Lewis wants you and the bike. My job is to make it happen."

Red Cap stepped into the conversation. "He knows what he's doing. Now show us how what you did to the bike."

Omar picked up the helmet, slipped it on for a few seconds then removed it, and held it under his left arm.

"Please continue."

"Okay, the bike. It was easier than the helmet partly because the tracker was an add-on."

He reached into the small gap between the fuel tank and seat with his index finger and gently lifted out the end of another red wire. "Pull this all the way and the tracker is off. Forever."

Then he turned to Red Cap. "He's all yours. I gotta get back to work."

As he walked away, Omar called out to him, "Hey, thanks. Any chance I'll see you again?"

"Not likely. Godspeed."

Red Cap took Omar into the shop office and briefed him on the timing for killing the trackers.

"Soon as it's dark, you need to ride out of here on the interstate west. There is a cell tower dead zone fifteen miles out. It's good for about another two miles. When you're sure you're in it, pull the wires and get off the highway. Go off-road south a-ways and you'll come to Route 66. Take it back east to town. When you see the sign for Route 99 take it south, under the railroad tracks. Just beyond the tracks on the left is an old barn. It's locked, so pull around the back and wait. I'll be making trips over there every thirty minutes until you get there. Any questions?"

Omar reached out and shook Red Cap's hand. "No, I got it. See you at the barn."

CHAPTER 35

Redeemers Clan, AZ

The men's compound was spread out along the creek north of the bridge. As soon as they arrived, Chet and Bruce were shown the tent they would share and given specific duties to perform. Chet was assigned to game hunting and power generation maintenance, while Bruce was given lookout and camp security duties under Lieutenant Marks.

Chet remained withdrawn, and Bruce honored the behavior by avoiding nonessential conversation. During the ten hours since their arrival, Chet had walked across the compound to the hospital tent every thirty minutes to see if Ruby had awakened.

Meals were shared in a small grassy open area called The Commons, which separated the men's and women's compounds. Everyone served themselves from steel pots hung over wood coals and plastic baskets of flatbread setting on a metal folding table. There were no other tables or chairs, only soft grass and tree stumps. It was during their evening meal that a nurse rushed over to Chet, bent down beside him, and whispered, "She's awake."

He stood so quickly that the rabbit stew he was about to eat spilled down the front of his pants and onto his boots. He brushed away pieces of meat and carrots, shook his boots, and followed her. The walk across The Commons and along the creek's edge to the hospital tent was the first time he had made the trek with any hope in his heart. His mind raced with thoughts of what to say and how to ask for her forgiveness.

When they reached the screened opening of the hospital tent, the sound of a dog howling somewhere in the distance stopped him in his tracks. He looked in the direction of the sound and remembered something Tom had told him.

God is like the Hound of Heaven. He will hunt for you until you find Him.

The nurse held the screened tent flap open for him and pointed to a cot deep in the long tent.

"Her cot is on the very end. She asked for Bruce and you."

Chet's words were soft and carried a tone of disappointment. "He's on duty somewhere."

Sheets hung along the path through the tent creating a white-walled corridor that ended at a large screen opening with a view of the creek and red rock cliff beyond. He walked slowly down the corridor, and as the breeze moved the sheets, he saw young girls resting peacefully on the same bunks they had been strapped to in the trailer. Tears trickled down his cheeks as release from guilt began to wash over him. Some had survived.

Ruby lay on her side facing the creek covered with a gray blanket. When she saw him stop at the foot of her cot, she slowly rolled over onto her back and pulled the blanket up to her chin. She beckoned him forward and smiled. Her smile and voice were soft and gentle like the love language of a new mother to her child.

"Oh, Chet."

The words and the love radiating from her face took his breath away and dropped him to his knees. She slipped her arm out from under the blanket and placed the palm of her hand against his cheek. The warmth of the gentle touch released the barriers in his mind and set him free to confess from his heart. The words came between sobs of joy and moans of grief.

"I am so sorry. Please forgive me."

She moved her hand under his chin and gently lifted his head up until their eyes locked.

"Chet, it is so beautiful. So real."

He wiped away tears with the back of his hand and waited for her to continue.

"Heaven. I saw Heaven."

She paused and looked deeply into his eyes.

"They are all there. My family, my friends, and the girl we helped."

Chet struggled to speak and managed only one word. "Girl?"

"Yes, she hugged me and thanked me. She said we saved her from the devil. She had found a message in her aunt's Bible that said Jesus would save and protect her. Heaven is real. God is real."

Chet remained stooped and speechless next to her cot.

Ruby whispered, "God told me you and Bruce will save many and angels will guide and protect you. It is called The Garnering, Chet. Like in the Bible when the poor found wheat left behind after the harvest."

Chet heard every word, and the riddle from Tom somehow seemed to be part of it all.

CHAPTER 36

Through the night and all the next morning, everything Ruby had said played over and over in Chet's head and tugged at his heart. Her description of Heaven and the angelic-like change to her persona were not in question, but her saying that God would use him and Bruce and the riddle in the message from Tom remained a mystery. He had seen Tom's personality change, like Ruby, after he found God. And for some reason he had kept Tom's last message.

God took the girl to Heaven because she read a message in a Bible. What if God was actually reaching out to him? What if Tom was right? What if Jesus loves him, even with all his failures? What if The Vanishing was actually God taking believers off the earth in a harvest of souls? What if the Hound of Heaven was pursuing him? What if Tom's message was a map to his future?

He held his hands over his head and spoke aloud to the empty tent.

"What if!"

Bruce was standing just outside the entrance of the tent with a cup of coffee in his hand watching the sunrise when he heard Chet's words. He turned, pushed the tent flap open, and asked, "What if what, buddy?"

Chet spun around and took the three steps needed to reach Bruce who leaned back in anticipation of a collision. Chet grabbed his shoulders with both hands.

"She is alive."

"I know. I was just there. The Heaven thing is really weird."

Chet released his hold, stepped back, and sat down on his cot. Bruce joined him inside and sat on his own cot across from Chet.

"Bruce, I'm sorry about blowing you off like I did. When I'm that pissed, I just shut down. It's better for everybody."

Bruce nodded in agreement. "Believe me, I understand. Apology accepted."

Chet reached under his cot, slid out the map case, and flipped it open.

"Want to show you something."

He reached in and pulled out his phone and notebook.

"I need you to listen to this message from a Christian friend of mine. I think he disappeared with all the others. Just listen and I'll tell you what I think it means."

Bruce kicked off his boots and leaned back on the cot with his feet up and his hands behind his head.

"Go."

After playing the message twice, Chet explained how the numbers were very likely coded latitude and longitude coordinates for a location in Albuquerque.

"That's all I've got so far. The 'Col, Vai' and 'under the cross down' part is still a mystery."

Bruce sat up on the edge of his cot.

"Ruby told me we are part of some kind of plan God has for saving people. You think this is part of it? Or something like that?"

"I do buddy…I do."

CHAPTER 37

Redeemers Clan, AZ

Captain Lewis stood on the bed of a pickup truck with three men standing behind him.

"Redeemers, we have new people I want you to meet."

The afternoon sun shone across The Commons that was filled with men and women, old and young, sixty in all. He reached over and tapped one of the men on the shoulder, inviting him to stand with him.

"This is Omar. Without him, many of the precious souls here and those recovering under the capable care of Dr. West and his staff would have been lost."

As was their custom, they raised their hands and rotated their wrists in silent applause.

Omar was dressed in faded blue jeans and a denim shirt that hung loosely on his small frame. His five-foot, seven-inch standing height was diminutive compared to Captain Lewis who stood over six feet, four inches tall in the riding boots he always wore.

He asked Omar to step back and tapped Chet and Bruce on the shoulders. The technique of doing so resembled that of a king knighting his soldiers.

They stood at the captain's right allowing room for Omar to stand on the left. Both men wore blue denim shirts and blue jeans, but unlike Omar, the fit enhanced Chet's tall lean frame and Bruce's broad torso that tapered to his waist.

"A few of you know these men. For those of you who were not part of the most recent redemption, this is Mr. Chet Rawlins and Mr. Bruce Coal. Fine men who took great risks passing though the Legion Compound and are now part of our clan. They have with them a highly qualified nurse who is currently in recovery after having braved untold hours locked inside the red trailer with the redeemed."

Mumbled whispers and nods of affirmation flowed through the crowd as they raised their hands in silent applause.

Jud was standing in the very back of the crowd and partially hidden behind a tree. He mumbled.

"Bullshit, I should be up there."

He then turned and walked toward to the women's compound and the hospital tent, both places of which he was forbidden. With everyone at The Commons and only a few nurses to worry about, he sensed an opportunity to check out the girls and find his little Indian hitchhiker. To avoid being seen, he followed the creek edge to the back wall of the hospital tent where he found a zippered access panel. Ever so slowly he lifted the tab hoping to slip in undetected.

He was stooped with his head and shoulders through the small opening when suddenly his feet were pulled out from under him. A pair of large strong hands had grasped his ankles and dragged him face down across the sandy gravel to the creek. He clawed at the ground and tried to kick his captor away but to no avail. At the water's edge he was grabbed by the neck and waist and thrown into the creek.

Lieutenant Marks brushed his hands together and watched Jud struggle to his feet in the knee-deep flowing water.

"Now get your ass over here and I'll try not to kill you today."

Lieutenant Marks and Jud had not seen the rider on a dark horse watching the event from his vantage point on the ridge above the creek.

*****

Verdicts were swift for those who violated Clan Law. Court was always held in The Commons after the evening meal, and everyone was required to attend.

Captain Lewis stood facing east on the bed of a pickup overlooking the audience. Jud stood next to Lieutenant Marks on the ground below, also facing the audience. It had taken Captain Lewis less than five minutes to deem Jud guilty on two counts.

"Jud Acres, you have been found guilty of two egregious offenses."

At that point Lieutenant Marks turned Jud around and ordered him to look up at the captain who then continued.

"Count One. Lying and dereliction of guard duty. To wit, you endangered camp safety when on lookout duty in the north blind. A duty to which you testified as having working knowledge of Morse code, when in fact you do not and, as such, compromised critical communications with outside contacts."

Jud shifted on his feet and attempted to lower his head when Lieutenant Marks placed the back of his hand under Jud's chin and pushed up until he was back in eye contact with Captain Lewis's stern bearded face.

"Count Two. Trespassing into restricted areas. To wit, you disregarded specific area restrictions and were apprehended while attempting to enter the women's ward in what is deemed to be of ill intent."

The captain nodded to Lieutenant Marks who then spun Jud around to face the audience.

The captain continued. "Your punishment shall be confinement and power generation for a period of not less than three months."

He then looked up and scanned the audience.

"Mr. Rawlins, please come forward."

Chet was caught completely off guard and looked at those standing around him before pushing his way forward though the crowd. When he was within two yards of Lieutenant Marks and Jud, the captain held out his hand as a stop signal.

"Mr. Rawlins, I am aware that you are trustworthy, that you have familiarity with Mr. Acres, and that you are assigned to oversee power generation. As such, I hereby assign you the tasks of overseeing Mr. Acre's punishment and assuring his confinement. Lieutenant Marks will assist with the initiation of the punishment and establishment of confinement."

Immediately Lieutenant Marks stepped toward Chet with Jud in tow.

"I'll keep him tonight. Meet me at breakfast and we'll set up the confinement at the power plant."

The crowd melted into the night leaving Chet alone with a thousand questions, not one of which could come out of his mouth.

Lieutenants Marks escorted Jud away as Captain Lewis approached.

"Thank you for that. It will benefit all."

"Actually, Captain, I'm in the dark."

The captain smiled and spoke as he walked away.

"You won't be in the morning. Good night, Mr. Rawlins."

CHAPTER 38

Redeemers Clan, AZ

The cool midnight breeze that flowed through the camp mingled with the gentle sounds of the creek created the illusion that all was well on the earth. Nothing could have been further from the truth.

Suicides and murders were rampant, leaving bodies to rot in apartments, homes, and vehicles. In the cities and suburbs, gangs looted and destroyed everything in their path.

Legion Enforcers apprehended dissentients, the infirmed, and the elderly and transported them to major cities for public execution. The method, location, and time for day were calculated by Capitia to create maximum fear and total submission to the One World Order and ultimately to Capitia itself.

Gray passenger buses with all but the driver's windows blacked out roamed the country collecting people held in Legion confinement for transportation to execution sites. One such bus was traveling east on the interstate bound for Albuquerque with scheduled stops in Barstow, Flagstaff, and Gallup.

Chet tossed and turned in his sleep as a nightmare played in his mind. He saw images of people weeping and clinging to each other in steel cages suspended and swinging mercilessly while deep, evil laughter filled the dark putrid air around them. He fought the dream and tried to force himself awake, but the scene would not stop.

Bruce, who was awakened by Chet's groans and movements, called out to him, "Chet, wake up."

Chet sat up in his cot and quickly hopped to his feet. The sweat running down his face and neck dripped onto his bare feet.

Bruce sat up and clicked on the lamp. "Looks like you had a night terror."

Chet sat back down on his cot, slowly shook his head from side to side, and whispered, "Oh my God. We're in hell."

Bruce had seen men with PTS awaken with night terrors. He knew it was best to let Chet come down slowly and at his own pace. Both men lay awake in silence for the remainder of the night.

Meanwhile, in the hospital tent, Ruby knelt next to her bunk praying. "Father, help me. I know now that Heaven is real. I don't want to stay here. Please take me back."

As she prayed, two forms like that of men, only taller and radiating light, stood beside her. It was the feeling of warmth near her body that caused her to open her eyes and look up. Before she could react, the Angel of Light to her left placed his hand on her shoulder and spoke softly, "Do not be afraid. We are here for your protection and guidance."

The Angel of Light on her right took her hand, helped her stand, and spoke in a gentle voice, "Rapha, we are here for you and the other chosen, Melek and Gibbor."

CHAPTER 39

Redeemers Clan, AZ

Lieutenant Marks held the coffee decanter up and asked, "More? You look like you need it."

Jud answered, "Yeah."

"Not you, asshole. I'm talking to your new master. How about it?"

Chet reached out, grasped the decanter, and poured coffee for himself, Jud, and Bruce.

Lieutenant Marks leaned back, patted his belly, and belched. "Nothing better than a good breakfast to kick-start the day."

He looked across the table where Jud was sitting between Chet and Bruce. "Better clean your plate, boy. You're going to need all the fuel you can pack in."

Jud started to speak, but Chet cut him off. "I don't like bein' kept in the dark. How exactly is this gonna work?"

Jud jumped into the conversation. "Yeah!"

Lieutenant Marks pointed his index finger at Jud's chest. "You, just shut up, watch, and obey. When we want to hear from you, we'll pull your chain, and I mean that literally."

He stood and leaned over the table with both palms flat on the table top. "Finish your coffee and bring him to the bridge. I'll meet you there."

After Lieutenant Marks was out of earshot, Chet turned to Jud. "I didn't ask for this, and I don't want it any more than you. So let's just do what he says and get this over with. I can be reasonable or I can be your worst enemy. Your call."

Bruce gave Chet a nod of approval, stood up, and grasped Jud's forearm. "Listen to the man and we'll all get along just fine."

By the time they reached the bridge, Lieutenant Marks had set up a harness and tether connected to the bridge footing. A rusty bicycle bolted to a steel platform stood nearby.

"Welcome, men."

He reached out, pulled Jud forward, spun him around, and buckled him into the harness. With an elastic tether draped over his hand, he pointed to the area between the bridge and the bicycle.

"This is your world. If you're thirsty, drink from the creek, and when you need to pee or crap"—he pointed to a wooden outhouse a tethers length away from the creek—"go there."

He glanced toward Chet to assure that he was following along and continued. "You will sleep under the bridge and food will be brought to you twice a day. That's the easy part. Now for the punishment."

He pointed to the rusty bicycle. "You will pedal that thing from sunrise to sunset. It's rigged to an alternator that charges the camp battery banks."

He then turned to Chet. "I'll be around to help if you need me. Any questions?"

Chet looked at Bruce and Jud, then back to Lieutenant Marks. "No, looks simple enough. I'm guessing he stays tethered like that for the whole three months."

"You've got it."

Then he looked at Jud. "Unless he gives us a reason to make things worse."

*****

Invisible and silent.

Those two words defined the methods of survival for the Redeemers Clan. The technique of silent applause Chet had seen at the meetings in The Commons opened his eyes to other invisible and silent systems around the camp.

Tents and vehicles were located under the cover of trees and draped with camouflage netting. Even the footpaths were kept dusted to blend in with the surrounding terrain.

The only open fire allowed was in The Commons where clan members tended the coals to assure that it never expired. The fire pit was covered with a steel frame for hanging cooking pots and cooking game on skewers. To control the smoke, a steel hood mounted on top of the frame captured it and distributed it through sheet metal vent pipes that radiated up and away. Its appearance was like that of a giant black upside-down octopus. Warm water was generated from copper pipes running inside the vents. Creek water was pushed by 12v marine pumps up to a chamber above the hood. From there, gravity pulled the water through the pipes in the vents and into an insulated water tank hidden under a tree near the creek.

Electrical power for the camp comprised of water-powered generators suspended from under the bridge into the flow of the creek. When the battery banks depleted, generator bicycles were ridden by volunteers, or as in Jud's case, by prisoners. Solar panels were out of the question because of the necessity to expose them to the sky.

The vehicles were intentionally covered with dust and mud for camouflage and additional mufflers had been added to the exhaust systems making them practically silent.

No noise-producing weapons were allowed, although Captain Lewis and Lieutenant Marks carried nine-millimeter pistols fitted with silencers. Other than those two pistols, the weapons inventory comprised of machetes, crossbows, and clubs. At least that was the case before Chet and Bruce arrived.

Chet was dressed in hunting gear and waterproof boots in preparation for his day to gather game as he walked from his tent to the Expedition hidden under a tree nearby. He lifted the rear hatch and slid a long black waterproof case within reach. Lieutenant Marks walked up the Expedition just as Chet pulled out one of the air rifles he and Bruce had taken from the men in Pagosa Springs.

"Whoa! What the hell are you doing?"

Chet turned quickly in the direction of the voice that came from the dim light of early morning.

"You scared the crap out of me. What I'm doin' is gettin' ready to kill some critters."

"Not with that you're not. Hand it over."

Chet opened the bolt, cradled the rifle in the palms of his hands, and presented it to him.

"It's an air rifle. Shoots tranquilizer darts. Should do the job."

"No sound? Really?"

Chet nodded his head and began to pull the rifle back when Lieutenant Marks grabbed it away.

"Can you guarantee me that it's silent?"

"Yep, test fired it right after we took it from some Breeder hunters."

"Got ammo?"

"Yeah, right here. Single-shot dart."

He took the dart from Chet's hand, slid it into the chamber, closed the bolt, and aimed rifle at Jud who was bent over washing his face in the creek.

Chet realized what was about to happen, but the dart left the barrel before he could respond. Jud flinched, stood up, rubbed his upper thigh, and turned toward the men. "What the fu…," and collapsed onto the sand.

Lieutenant Marks handed the rifle back to Chet and spoke as he walked toward Jud's limp body.

"Looks like it works. Good hunting."

CHAPTER 40

Chevelon Canyon, AZ

"Friend or foe?"

Chet recognized Bruce's voice but had no clue where he was hiding.

"Friend. Show yourself."

The scrub bushes behind Chet rustled and Bruce steeped out onto the gravel road.

"Hey, buddy, glad you came by. Looks like your goin' huntin'."

Chet slipped the air rifle from his shoulder and patted the stock. "Remember these?"

"Sure do. Glad you got it because we've got a mountain lion roaming around here. By the looks of his tracks, I'm guessing sixty maybe eighty pounds."

He pointed up the road to the muddy outfall of a roadside spring. "Fresh tracks when I got here a couple hours ago. I think he was drinkin' at the spring and I spooked him."

Chet slid a dart into the chamber and closed the bolt. Then with a chuckle he said, "Marks shot Jud with this thing. Now we're down to three darts."

Bruce bent over laughing and exclaimed, "Shot him? Really?"

"Really! Don't know how long he'll be out. Guess we'll find out when we get back to camp."

Chet slung the rifle over his shoulder and headed up the road toward the spring, and Bruce disappeared back into the south blind, still chuckling.

When Chet reached the spring, he noticed several tracks in the mud, some from a mountain lion and other smaller tracks like those of a wolf or dog. He climbed up the low embankment next to the spring outfall and found a hiding place deeper in the forest but within shooting range of the air rifle.

A few minutes after settling in he heard what sounded like heavy panting somewhere in the thicket behind him. He felt the unmistakable feeling of being watched and slowly turned to face the direction of the sound. The rifle was in firing position, and his finger was resting on the trigger when the panting stopped and the bushes came alive with motion. A mountain lion exploded out of the brush coming straight for him. He rolled to the side and ducked behind a pine tree as the lion shot past him and continued on in pursuit of something running through the forest beyond.

A yelping sound filled the air. Through the thicket he could see the mountain lion standing over something pinned to the ground under its huge, front paw. It was the perfect shot and he took it. The lion dropped like a rock.

He pulled his hunting knife from its holster and rushed through the brush to finish the kill. There on the ground lying under the mountain lion's shoulder was a dog. At first it did not move, but as he knelt down to get a closer look, the dog's eyes opened and his tail quivered.

Chet rolled the big cat over onto its back and cut its throat. He holstered his hunting knife and slowly moved his hand toward the dog's snout. The closer his hand came toward the dog the more the quivering tail began to wag.

"Hey there, boy. That was a close one."

In response, his shaggy tail wagged slightly faster. He lifted his head and slowly moved his snout closer to Chet's open hand.

⸎⸎⸎⸎⸎

The sight of the two men walking across the bridge toward The Commons was like none they had ever seen. The muscular, shorter man carried the limp body of a mountain lion draped over his shoulders. Next to him walked a taller man with long red hair and a shaggy brown dog limping along at his side. It was not until they reached the edge of The Commons that they were recognized.

Bruce walked over to the fire pit where women were preparing the evening meal and dropped the big cat onto the ground.

"Not sure how to cook this but I'll help skin it. We need a rug in our tent."

Chet and the dog stopped at the base of the bridge where Jud lay passed out on his cot. The dog moved cautiously closer, sniffed Jud's hand, and let out a low deep growl. The sound startled Jud awake and he fell off the cot onto the sand at Chet's feet.

"What the hell!"

The dog moved closer to Chet and growled at Jud, again.

"Looks like he doesn't like you."

Jud sat up in the sand and rub his temples as he spoke. "I hate dogs, and my head's killin' me."

He scanned his surrounding with a puzzled look on his face. "How did I get here? Last thing I remember was something bit me."

Chet chuckled as he and the dog turned and walked away.

"Don't know, but you better get on that bike before Marks sees you loafin'."

He walked the short distance to his tent with the dog following close behind.

When Bruce arrived at the tent, he saw Chet sitting on a stump nearby with the dog curled up at his feet. He called out from a few yards away.

"How about namin' him Hound Dog."

Chet looked in Bruce's direction and nodded his head. "Not bad. Dog for short."

He reached down and continued brushing Dog's shaggy brown coat. "The cat scratched him on the rump, otherwise looks like he's okay."

Bruce squatted down on his heels, Indian style, rubbed Dog's head, and changed the subject.

"Ruby is up and around. I saw her on the way here. What say we go for a visit?"

CHAPTER 41

Redeemers Clan, AZ

They had changed in so many ways since the mountains of Colorado, and Ruby was the first to acknowledge it.

She was sitting on the grass in The Commons when they found her. Her shimmering black hair was brushed smooth and lay against the shoulders of her gray gown. The late afternoon sun was at her back and created a glow around her hair and face. She sat with her knees pulled up against her breasts. Her arms were wrapped around her folded legs, holding them in place.

Bruce stood, leaning against a tree, and admired her almost angelic face and eyes as she spoke.

"Bruce, your full beard and long hair is an amazing transformation. Earlier when you called out to me, I almost didn't recognize you. But God showed me that you are Gibbor, God's warrior for The Garnering."

She seemed at complete peace, which was miraculous considering what she had been through and the state of the world. Maybe she had forgotten about The Vanishing, the Enforcers, her ordeal in the trailer, and the dead girl…and now God is talking to her.

"Chet, you have lost your joy and your confidence. I saw when you first came to me last week that your heart is broken, but Chet, you have a purpose ahead. A purpose that Angels of Light will show you in pieces over time. You are Melek, God's sovereign for The Garnering."

She looked over at Dog and patted the grass next to her feet. He crept over and curled up beside her. She rested her hand on top of his head and continued. "I have the Heavenly name Rapha. Healer for The Garnering."

Bruce looked over at Chet and wondered what he would say.

Ruby continued. "Captain Lewis has given me a Bible and is teaching me things. He said that our Heavenly names Melek, Gibbor, and Rapha are from the ancient Hebrew language. The Vanishing was meant to be; he called it the Rapture. We are living in the time called the Great Tribulation and many will die, but Captain Lewis said if we stay hidden and don't take the Mark of the Beast, we will live."

Chet slowly stood up, looked deeply into her eyes, and walked away without speaking a word. The brief mental connection they shared told her enough. He was overwhelmed, but he understood. Dog hopped up to follow him but stopped and stayed with Ruby.

Bruce and Ruby watched Chet go and Ruby spoke first. "Stay close to him. You are his only worldly friend and his protector. I love you both and God loves you even more."

Bruce folded his arms across his chest and let out a deep sigh. He could not say what he was thinking, so he simply nodded and walked away in the direction Chet had gone.

Ruby watched him go, laid her head on her knees, and prayed. "Father, help me, help them, help us."

*****

When Bruce reached the tent, he found Chet sitting on the floor studying maps and reading his notes from Tom's message. The frustration Bruce felt echoed from his voice as he spoke out the words he wanted to say to Ruby but could not.

"Jesus, Chet! What happened to her? God? Really? If there is a good God then why in hell do good people and babies die? Why is there war? How can young girls get hunted down like animals for breeding? Why…?"

His voice trailed off as he turned to leave.

"I can't tell you. Sit down, we need to talk."

He stopped, looked down at Chet, and spoke two words in a resigned tone. "About what?"

"What she said and how she's right. I've never told you about my past or the things I did and the decisions I made that I now know were wrong. All because I doubted God, just like you. Now sit."

Bruce sat down on his cot.

Chet put the maps and notebook back into the map case and sat on his cot facing Bruce.

"I had a friend, two friends really, who tried to get me hooked up with God and a project that I think was part of The Vanishing, the Rapture, like Ruby called it. I was the flight instructor for an architect named David Adams and he offered me a job as his corporate pilot. About that same time, I got a chance to get on with Continental Airlines and I took it. A friend of mine was looking for a flying job, so I got them together. My friend's name was Thomas Winslow. The message and riddle we talked about was from Tom, Thomas Winslow."

Bruce lay back on his cot.

"Keep going."

Chet leaned forward with his elbows on his knees and looked down at his hands, as though preparing to read from a script.

"David, the architect, died in a plane crash, and his pilot, Tom, was busted up but survived. I did some things to protect Tom from the FAA investigation. Things they didn't like, so they took my license and I lost my job. So, I bought the truck and picked up where my daddy left off. Truckin'. I was eleven when he died, and I blamed God. My daddy was one of the good people and God took him. So, I get it, I know how you feel."

He paused and looked up at Bruce. "But we're wrong. People die, babies die, bad things happen to good people, and it's not God's fault. It's God's plan."

Bruce sat up and put his feet on the floor. "His plan?"

"Yeah, his plan."

"You're not making me like the God thing!"

"I'm not trying to. But I need your help finding 'Col and Vai under the cross down.' I think it's one of the project locations David and Tom were building, and I think it has something to do with The Vanishing."

Bruce put his right hand on Chet's shoulder.

"I'll help. You know I will, but what are we looking for, considering the risk?"

"I'm not sure yet. But I know it's something we need to do. Once we find it, we can decide whether it was worth it. Or not."

Bruce shook his head slowly and asked, "Gibbor? Melek? What is she talking about?"

Chet's answer was spoken with calm authority, "The Garnering."

CHAPTER 42

"Men, I have called you together this morning for a new mission. News has reached us of a bus loaded with people scheduled for execution. These are not criminals; on the contrary, these are merely innocent civilians. The bus is traveling from Flagstaff with its final destination to a city where the people are scheduled to be executed, Albuquerque."

Captain Lewis paused and scanned the small group of men standing before him. Good men, strong men, and most importantly, trustworthy men. The pride he felt for them and for his role in saving the people projected with the words he spoke.

"This is a unique opportunity, albeit a difficult one. We need two teams working in unison. Team Alpha will commandeer the bus, and Team Omega will collect and transport the captives to the camp. As always, coordination and timing are paramount."

He scanned the group and called Omar forward. Then he pointed at Chet and Bruce who were standing in front of the group.

"Mr. Rawlins and Mr. Coal, please come forward."

They made the few steps forward necessary to stand next to the captain and Omar.

The captain then addressed the group. "Having considered the abilities of these three men, it has been decided that they are to be Team Alpha."

He turned his back to the audience and spoke to Chet, Bruce, and Omar in a low voice. "I leave the method of commandeering the bus and safely transporting the captives to the rendezvous location up to you. You will bring the bus and captives to the Winslow truck stop where Team Omega will take over. I will advise you of the rendezvous time. Go now and plan your attack. Godspeed."

*****

Chet, Bruce, and Omar had just finished working out the attack plan for the assault on the bus when Lieutenant Marks pulled open the tent flap and announced his arrival.

"Captain Lewis instructed me to come by and hear your plan."

Chet spoke up first. "Good. We're at a point where we can fill you in."

Chet moved over to make room on his cot. As seated, Chet and Lieutenant Marks sat opposite and facing Bruce and Omar who were sitting on Bruce's cot. The Enforcer's suit and helmet Omar had brought to the camp lay on the floor at their feet. Chet pointed to the suit and began his description of the plan.

"This thing fits Omar and he knows how to use it. With it and the motorcycle, we'll set up a fake crash scene to get the bus to stop. I'll be down the road a bit with one of the clan's pickups. Then, as the bus approaches the crash scene, I'll drive straight at the bus with my lights flashin'. We figure that seein' the crash and a pickup swerving toward 'em on the wrong side of the road should stop 'em. This will all happen in a cell tower dead zone that Omar knows about."

Chet nodded toward Bruce. "Your turn."

Bruce turned slightly toward Lieutenant Marks and began. "Chet will drive the pickup; Omar will be in the suit and lying on the ground along the side of the road. And the motorcycle will be out in middle of the road. I'll be laying low in a ditch near to Omar."

Bruce nodded toward Omar. "Your turn."

Omar picked up the suit and began. "This suit is fully functional except for the tracking feature, which, as you know, has been disabled along with the tracker on the motorcycle. In case the Enforcers on the bus wear their helmets when they approach me, I will be lying face down."

Lieutenant Marks interrupted, "Why face down?"

Omar set the suit down and picked up the helmet. "Enforcer's suits have no identification or rank insignias that can be seen with the naked eye. However, the helmets are fitted with lenses that allow the suit marking to be seen."

Bruce interjected, "And that is a big problem we need to avoid because Lieutenant Omar is AWOL. We're sure there's a warrant out for him."

Omar continued, "It is our belief that they will bend down and attempt to roll me over. When they do, this will happen."

He set the helmet down and picked the suit up by one of its sleeves.

"The suits are equipped with several defense features including this one."

He held the sleeve by the wrist opening and aimed it at the tent flap. Immediately a beam of intense light showed on the tent flap causing the men to shield their eyes.

"This fires from both sleeves. So when they bend down, I will roll over and light up their faces, whether they have helmets on or not."

Lieutenant Marks asked, "How will you know when to roll over? You'll be face down."

Omar pointed to the helmet. "Rear imaging feature."

"Holy crap. I had no idea."

Omar nodded toward Bruce who continued the briefing. "When Omar blinds them, I'll take 'em down from behind. Omar has shown us their Achilles's heel. Turns out there's a kill switch on the back of the suit where it joins the helmet. I'll shut 'em down before they see it comin'. They won't see without taking the helmets off or flipping up the face masks. And none of their weapons will work."

Then he held out his right hand, palm up, exposing three tranquilizer darts.

"I figure that is a pretty good time to put them asleep with these."

Lieutenant Marks nodded his approval but then asked, "What if the driver stays in the bus?"

Chet responded, "I'll have the pickup stopped in front of him."

"And he might just drive through you. Better let me take care of the driver." He smiled and looked at Chet. "I wouldn't want to lose one of our pickups."

He glanced at his watch, stood up, and waved his index finger at Chet and Bruce.

"Captain Lewis wants you two to meet him at the hospital tent. You've got ten minutes."

Bruce stood and asked, "About our plan?"

Lieutenant Marks shrugged his shoulders. "Don't know. Just don't be late."

He walked over to the tent flap, held it open, and turned to face them. "I like the plan. Captain Lewis will give you our departure time, and I will let the captain know that I'm on Team Alpha with you."

He was out of the tent before they could respond.

Bruce patted Omar on the shoulder. "Looks like you dodged gettin' called before the captain. We'll meet you after and finalize the small stuff."

Omar nodded in agreement, gathered up the suit and helmet, and spoke as he exited the tent, "I will be in my tent."

As Chet and Bruce walked through The Commons, Bruce noticed the mountain lion carcass turning slowly on a spit over a massive heap of hot coals. He was surprised that he had not been included in skinning the beast.

"What the hell. I told them I wanted the hide for our tent."

As they walked on, Chet placed his left hand on Bruce's shoulder and spoke, "We may not need it."

Bruce turned causing Chet's hand to fall away. "What? Why?"

Chet whispered the answer, "Because we probably aren't comin' back."

CHAPTER 43

As Chet and Bruce neared the hospital tent, they noticed Captain Lewis and Ruby sitting in chairs around a small folding table set up on the beach at the edge of the creek. The air was filled with the scent of the forest and the gentle sounds of the flowing creek.

Captain Lewis saw them and waved them over with a hand gesture. Ruby, with Dog curled up at her feet, smiled warmly as they approached.

The captain stood and gestured toward two empty chairs at the table.

"Gentlemen, please sit. Thank you for coming and for being punctual."

He sat back down and waited for them to be seated. Lying on the table before him were three leather-bound books. One large and brown, one smaller and gray, and the other much smaller, pocket-sized and black.

Everyone sat in silence for several seconds, which felt like hours to Bruce. The pregnant silence was washed away by Ruby's soft voice.

"I am so grateful for you two. You took me in when I was alone. You defended me when I was in danger, and you transported me to safety when I was helpless."

She paused to wipe a tear away and continued, "It is very important that you listen to what the captain and I are going to share with you. Please keep your hearts open to receive."

She then reached over and slid the little black book toward Chet.

"This is yours now. Guard it, read it, and believe what God teaches you from it."

Chet recognized it as a Bible and placed his right hand over it. "I will. I promise."

Bruce sat in silence uncertain of what was transpiring before his eyes. He noticed that Ruby's face seemed to glow softly and that Chet seemed to understand what was happening.

Captain Lewis placed both hands on the table with the large brown Bible resting between them. He then leaned closer to the men.

"God has made it clear to us that you are more than who you think you are. You are in fact called to do for the lost that which you have done for Ruby. Let me reiterate the words for you."

He paused, placed both hands over his Bible, and continued, "You will gather those who have been left behind. You will defend those who are in danger, and you will transport those who are helpless to safety."

Chet listened intently and nodded in agreement. His voice was stern and confident. "I understand."

Ruby reached out and placed her left hand over Chet's and gestured for Bruce's hand. He complied and she placed her right hand over his.

"There is more to tell you. Please listen carefully and believe."

She looked toward Captain Lewis who nodded as if granting permission for her to continue.

"I was visited by two angelic beings. They were dispatched from Heaven to guide and protect us. They were with us the day we met on the mountain and they have been with us every day since."

Bruce tried to speak but could not. Ruby saw him struggling to speak and smiled.

"You will be allowed to speak in time, but not yet. You see, they are here with us. One has his hand over your mouth and will release you after you have received."

Bruce's mind was spinning with questions of God, Angels, and the reality that he was, in fact, muted!

Ruby continued with her hands still resting on the men's hands.

"The Angels did not give me their names, but they did tell me ours."

Chet and Bruce felt the temperature of her hands increasing as she spoke.

"God has called us and has named us."

She increased the pressure on Chet's hand.

"As you may remember from our meeting in The Commons, you, Chet, are Melek, the Leader."

Then Bruce felt her hand pressed harder on his.

"You are Gibbor, the Warrior, and I am Rapha, the Healer."

The normally commanding voice of Captain Lewis flowed gently into the conversation, like that of a grandfather speaking to his grandchildren.

"Those names and their meanings are from the ancient Hebrew language. God has revealed His Heavenly purpose to you and has dispatched His Angels to be with you. Furthermore, you are empowered with the Gifts of the Spirit as described in the book of First Corinthians, Chapter Twelve."

Chet did not speak and Bruce could not.

Captain Lewis stood, walked around behind the men, and placed his hands on their shoulders. As he did, Ruby moved her hands from theirs, stood, and leaned closer to them.

"'I love and empower you,' says the Lord."

As she spoke, she placed her finger tips onto their foreheads. What appeared to the men to be bright light and soft warmth washed over them as they slowly tipped backward in their chairs. Captain Lewis cradled them and gently lowered them to the ground.

CHAPTER 44

Redeemers Clan, AZ

Bruce pushed back the gray wool blanket from his face and sat up on his cot. He looked around the tent and saw Chet standing near the tent flap and looking down at him. He waited a few moments before exclaiming, "Whoa, what a weird dream I had!"

Chet calmly replied, "You weren't dreamin'."

Bruce sat up on the edge of his cot and gave Chet a puzzled look.

"Okay, I was afraid of that. But how did I get here?" he said while pointing to his cot.

Chet picked up Bruce's empty duffel bag and tossed it on the cot. "Fireman's carry. Pack up, we move out in thirty minutes."

"Come on, Chet, talk to me."

"In the truck on the way to the setup."

Then he turned and left the tent, leaving Bruce almost as confused as he had been when he awoke.

Chet, Omar, and Lieutenant Marks were loading the motorcycle into the pickup bed when Bruce arrived with his duffel bag over his shoulder. Of the four men, only Chet and Bruce knew what had transpired the night before.

Bruce tossed his duffel bag into the truck bed and turned to Chet. "I remember what happened until Ruby touched me on the forehead, and I remember what she and Captain Lewis said about our mission and God and even our names. But I don't know what to do with it."

"I've got that part. You just follow our plan and you'll get a better idea of where we go from here. Remember the riddle, the map, and Albuquerque?"

Bruce nodded. "Yeah."

"If this setup works, the bus is ours. And we're takin' it to Albuquerque."

*****

At exactly 7:19 pm, an unmarked gray OWO bus crested the hill and began its descent into the cell phone dead zone on Interstate 40 seventeen miles west of Winslow, Arizona. It was manned by two Enforcers and carried six prisoners locked inside steel cages suspended from rails on the ceiling. The Enforcers were separated from the lock-up by a steel wall just behind the driver and front passenger seats. The wall had two purposes: one was for security and the other was to block the stench of feces and urine that pooled on the floor under the cages.

The flashing lights of a vehicle in the distance coming at them on the wrong side of the road caused them to reduce speed.

"What the hell?"

"Hey, looks like a bike in the road."

"And an Enforcer down next to it."

The driver slowed the bus to a stop in the fast lane next to the crash scene.

"Check it out."

"Okay, call it in."

"Can't get a signal. Just do it and hurry."

The driver remained helmetless and the other Enforce pulled on his helmet before opening the door and stepping out. The dirt-covered pickup truck that had been driving toward them with its lights flashing stopped directly in front of the bus and turned off its lights.

The next series of events occurred within seconds of each other, none of which the Enforcers expected.

Omar lay face down in the Enforcer's suit next to the motorcycle. The Enforcer stepped out of the bus and knelt down intending to roll him over. Suddenly Omar moved and blinded him with the intense lights projecting from the suit's sleeves. At that very moment, Chet flashed on the pickup truck's headlights causing the bus driver to hold his right hand over his eyes. The light pouring in through the bus windshield gave Lieutenant Marks the light he needed to get a clear shot. The muffled pop of Lieutenant Marks 9mm pistol sent a bullet blasting through the bus driver's side window and into the temple of the helmetless Enforcer. The blinded Enforcer popped open his face mask only to have a needle jabbed into his exposed face just below the cheekbone. Bruce held him from behind as he collapsed from the tranquilizing agent pumping into his brain.

A rider on a dark horse watched the scene from a secluded vantage point. He waited in silence until the motorcycle and bus drove away, then continued on to the next stop of his journey.

CHAPTER 45

Team Omega had traveled during the night and was safely hidden inside of the huge truck repair bays in the Winslow truck stop. Red Cap was seated in the café drinking coffee and watching for Team Alpha to pull off the interstate with the bus. He watched and prayed.

"Lord, please bring them safely to us. We can't do this without You."

At the conclusion of his short silent prayer, he saw an Enforcer on a motorcycle approaching from the Highway 66 side of the truck stop lot. The motorcycle rolled onto the lot and continued around to the back of the building. He hoped and believed that it was Omar. The desire to go to the shop and see if it was true was strong, but his orders were to stay in the café, watch for the bus and any unexpected Legion troops or equipment.

His wait was not long. Within five minutes a gray OWO bus exited the interstate, rolled down the off-ramp, and onto the truck stop lot with a dirty pickup truck following close behind. They too continued around the building.

The bay doors were rolled up and back down as soon as the vehicles were fully inside. Red Cap came into the truck bay and joined Captain Lewis, Omar, and Ruby who stood nearby waiting for the bus door to open.

Bruce was the first to disembark the bus and did so with a smile and thumbs-up signal.

"Went like clockwork."

Before he could continue, Chet stepped off the bus and interjected, "Six souls. It stinks bad in there but they're alive."

Captain Lewis approached the men. "And the Enforcers?"

Lieutenant Marks walked up and answered, "Two. One dead, one asleep."

Captain Lewis lowered his head and spoke softly, "Unfortunate but necessary I am sure."

Lieutenant Marks nodded in the affirmative.

With a quick change in demeanor, Captain Lewis began issuing orders to the clansmen waiting by clan vehicles lined up in the adjacent bay. Several clansmen rushed into the bus with tools, buckets of hot water, and blankets. Others carried the bodies of the Enforcers from the cab of the bus and laid them on a worktable. With great efficiency and under the guidance of Omar, they stripped the men of their uniforms and covered their bodies with blankets. A small hole in the left temple of one of the bodies made it obvious which one was dead and which one was tranquilized. As a precaution, they tapped his mouth closed and hog-tied him with rope.

When Captain Lewis was confident that the cleanup and loading was underway, he signaled for Chet to join him in the supervisor's office.

"Chet, our experience together and this victory over evil has confirmed to me that now is the appropriate time to share my past with you and how the Redeemers Clan came to be. In a dream, I saw the chaos to which we are now surrounded. In the dream an Angel called me Melek and Lieutenant Marks, Gibbor. When I awoke, I studied the Hebrew dictionary and confirmed the meanings. I…we are to lead with the help and protection of our Gibbor, our warriors. At the time I did not fully understand the reason for or the depth of the task.

He paused briefly and continued, "Before The Vanishing, I was a professor of World Religions at NAU, Northern Arizona University, and Lieutenant Marks, a retired Army officer, was head of campus security. I told him of my dream and he confessed that he had a similar dream…hence, the Redeemers Clan.

"It was not until Ruby's encounter with the Angels of Light that I realized the full power and authority to which God has entrusted us. I believe God is dispatching Angels and empowering leaders with warriors to gather and protect the lost all over the world."

Bruce entered the office and spoke in an urgent tone, "The people are loaded in the SUVs. The dead guy is in one of the pickups. What do we do with the live one?"

Chet answered, "I've got plans for both of them. Hold tight, I'll be there in a minute."

Then he offered his hand to Captain Lewis who grasped it and completed the handshake.

Captain Lewis spoke first, "Godspeed, Melek."

Chet nodded, left the office, and found Bruce standing by the hog-tied Enforcer still lying unconscious on the worktable.

"Don't know how long he'll be out."

Chet answered, "Have some people to put him and the dead one back in the bus in separate cages."

Time was running out, yet serious technical tasks had to be completed before they could get the bus back on the road.

Chet and Bruce listened intently as Omar explained and demonstrated how to don and operate the suits they had removed from the captured Enforcers. Each man had a suit on the ground before them, including Omar. As he demonstrated, Chet and Bruce followed each instruction with their respective suits.

"Step in and pull the suit up until you can get our arms into the sleeves then put it on as you would a coat. You will notice that it will feel too large."

Both men followed the instruction and waited.

"Now, close the front flap and feel across your chest with your left hand until you find a raised patch located on your right pectoral muscle. Embedded in the patch is an activation switch that, when pressed, shrinks the suit to your body. Don't worry, there are pressure sensors that control the fit."

The men pressed the patches and the suits shrunk to a comfortable formed fit. Bruce spoke out in amazement, "Wow, this is great!"

Omar smiled as he spoke, "You haven't seen anything yet. Now open the helmet's facemask and pull the helmets on."

They complied and stood waiting for more instructions. Omar then pulled on his helmet, also with the facemask opened.

"This next step will activate all of the suit's systems. I only have time to explain the basics. The suits operate on voice commands spoken within the helmet so you will be able to experiment on your own."

He chuckled and continued, "Just be careful where you point the sleeves."

Bruce interrupted with a question, "What powers these things? Do we need to charge batteries of something?"

"No. The suit operates on heat generated by your body, which fuels small fusion reactors in the boots. There is a small battery for power until your heat source kicks in."

Bruce exclaimed, "Fusion reactors!"

While Chet and Bruce continued their training, other important tasks were being carried out.

The truck stop mechanic named Jerry, who had disabled the tracking devices on Omar's motorcycle and suit, was busy preparing the bus. He installed an on/off switch on the bus's tracking device, replaced the left rear outer tire, and modified the repair logbook to justify the delay.

Ruby and Captain Lewis attended to the two women and four men resting in the SUVs. While Ruby checked them for injuries, Captain Lewis explained that they were safe and would soon be an important part of the Redeemers Clan.

On the other side of the truck bays, clansmen loaded fifty-pound bags of potatoes, apples, and carrots into the pickups. So far, the café had successfully provided food for the Clan without being discovered.

Unnoticed by most, but with great effect, Dog curled up at the feet of the two women huddled together in one of the clan's SUVs. His keen ability to soothe their fear was evident when they leaned over to pet him and smiled for the first time since being captured, judged, and sentenced to death by beheading.

Outside and above the truck stop the illuminating power of three Angels of Light held a gathering presence of evil at bay.

CHAPTER 46

Truck Stop, Winslow, AZ

Lieutenant Marks and three clansmen had loaded the bodies of the naked Enforcers into separate cages in the bus. It was during the loading process that they discovered how the cage system operated. Each cage was suspended from a common rail system that ran from the front bulkhead to the back of the bus where double doors opened to allow loading and offloading. The final link of the rail was detachable and connected to a hydraulic winch. There were a total of eight cages in the system, two of which now held the captured Enforcers.

Lieutenant Marks looked around and spotted Chet and Bruce, who were getting accustomed to their Enforcers suits. He walked briskly to his pickup and pulled Jud out of the cab.

"You're coming with me."

Jud would have resisted, but the tape wrapped over his mouth and the rope that restrained his wrists behind his back made it impossible. Lieutenant Marks grabbed him by the wrists and steered him toward Chet and Bruce who saw them coming. Bruce spoke first, "What the hell is he doin' here?"

Lieutenant Marks pushed Jud onto a steel chair next to the men. "He's yours. He cut the tether and took off last night. Captain Lewis sent Dog out to track him and they found him hiding behind the north security shack.

Bruce started to object, but Chet cut him off. "We'll take him."

Bruce looked at Jud and then at Chet. "How's this gonna work?"

Chet nodded toward the bus then looked directly at Jud. "The bus had six in cages and now it'll have three. We'll add a note to the

155

logbook that shows two women and one man died en route, and the bodies were dumped."

Jud attempted to stand and Chet stopped him with a raised hand. "Sit!"

Chet turned to Lieutenant Marks. "Load him."

PART FOUR
Albuquerque

CHAPTER 47

West of Legion Compound, Gallup, NM

The new commander of the Gallup Legion Compound was acutely aware of the failure and self-inflicted death of his predecessor. He was equally aware of the havoc, a problem now facing him, could create if news of it reached Capitia. The problem was a missing OWO bus carrying six prisoners bound for execution in Albuquerque. It was behind schedule and had not been found with tracking equipment. He was about to send out a second drone and a squad of Enforcers to hunt it down when the voice of his staff assistant came over the office intercom.

"Sir, we have picked up a tracking signal on the missing prison bus and it has been visually confirmed by drone. Inbound, ETA thirty minutes."

He placed both hands on the desktop and leaned toward the intercom. "Send an escort and prepare the prisoners."

"Yes, sir."

The tracking signal became active when Bruce flipped it on with the kill switch mechanic Jerry had hidden under the passenger seat. They had intentionally waited to turn on the tracking signal at a location as far from the truck stop as possible. Both men were in their Enforcer's suits with helmets on and face masks open. They had used the helmet facemasks to see insignias and name tags of the suits and discovered that Enforcers were identified by alphanumeric designations. Chet's suit bore the name T-9 and Bruce's was T-12.

Jud and the surviving Enforcer were naked, bound, gagged, and sitting calmly in their cages with black mesh bags secured over their heads. Omar had shown them the bags and explained that the mesh was impregnated with a sleeping agent to subdue unruly or hysterical prisoners.

The caged body of the dead Enforcer was stuffed inside a brown body bag emblazoned with a bright orange quarantine label.

Bruce noticed the drone flying next to the bus on passenger side.

"That didn't take long."

Chet glanced in the direction of the drone. "If that thing moves in front, we need to get the masks down."

Bruce pointed to the road ahead and answered, "Or now!"

The two vehicle escorts dispatched by the checkpoint commander were one-half mile ahead and crossing the dirt median to merge with the bus.

*****

The three-vehicle convoy slowed to a stop at the iron gate of the Gallup Compound west entrance. Chet and Bruce remained in the bus as the driver of the armored troop carrier ahead of them dismounted and walked the short distance to the gate shack.

Chet watched in the side mirror as the other armored troop carrier pulled out from behind the bus and drove forward, stopping next to the lead vehicle.

Chet's voice was modulated by the speaker system of his closed helmet. The resulting words carried a robotic, nonhuman, masculine sound. "You good?"

The sound of Bruce's voice spoken through his suit's system closely matched that of Chet's. "Yeah. Looks like a good time for me to get in the back."

Chet nodded in agreement.

Bruce placed his left hand on the bulkhead door lever and his right hand on Chet's shoulder. "Good thing these suits have re-breathers. I'm guessin' it still stinks back there."

"Go! Their comin' this way."

Bruce quickly pulled the bulkhead door open and ducked inside, intentionally leaving it ajar as planned. By the time the approaching pair of Enforcers reached the bus the stench of raw human waste had filled the bus cab. One of the Enforcers stopped at the bus door and the other stayed back a few feet. The Enforcer at the door, whose face mask was up, rapped his gloved fist on the glass panel of the door and shouted, "Open up!"

Chet grasped the door actuator and pulled. The stench in the cab spilled out and hit the unprotected faces of the Enforcers. Both of them turned away from the source and quickly pulled down their face masks. While remaining several feet away, they turned back to face the bus door.

The Enforcer who had rapped on the door called out to Chet. His voice carried by the robotic speech of his suit. "Damn! What the hell happened in there?"

Chet remained in the driver's seat with his mask down. "Yeah, we've got a mess in here."

"Where's your shotgun?"

Chet paused and then realized that he was asking about Bruce. "He's in the back. Get us to the fuel dock ASAP, we're behind schedule."

The second Enforcer answered, "No shit. No, wait, you already did."

His remark caused both Enforcers to laugh at the sick humor as they walked back to their vehicles.

Chet rapped on the bulkhead wall and called out to Bruce. "All clear."

He was pulling the bus door closed as Bruce joined him in the cab. Bruce pushed the bulkhead door closed and set the latch.

"We got a problem back there."

"Tell me."

Bruce sat down in the passenger seat and reached up to open his face mask.

Chet quickly responded, "Not yet. What's up back there?"

Bruce obeyed and answered with the suit's voice, "The body bag is inflating. The guy's getting ripe."

"Go back there and open the zipper a few inches. The added stink will help isolate us little longer."

Bruce moved toward the bulkhead door. "Then what?"

"Don't know. Just got to take it a step at a time. We fuel up and we get out of here, that's next. Are the other two still out?"

"They are. And if they wake up, they'll wish they hadn't."

Chet nodded toward the gate. "We're rollin'. Open the bag and stay back there till I call you."

Bruce complied without speaking.

Chet followed the troop carriers toward the opened gate. One continued on and the other stopped just beyond the gate. Chet pulled up behind and saw an Enforcer standing between the guard shack and the bus door. Chet opened the bus door and waited for him to speak first. With his face mask down, he could see the Enforcers name tag, G-39.

"Where's your shotgun?"

"In the back."

"Need to see him. Need your IDs."

Chet banged on the bullhead with his fist. "T-12. Get up here."

Bruce had been listening from just behind the bulkhead door and shouted back, "What?"

Chet played into the disrespectful tone of Bruce's response. "Get your ass up here!"

Bruce abruptly pushed the bulkhead door open and leaned into the cab far enough for the Enforcer to see his name tag. Fortunately, seeing their name tags satisfied the demand to see their IDs. The Enforcer gave a hand signal to the driver of the troop carrier then instructed Chet, T-9, to follow it to the fuel dock.

At that very moment three naked male prisoners ages twenty-two to twenty-five were being moved from their holding pen into separate steel cages, cages that would be moved to the fuel dock and loaded onto the bus.

CHAPTER 48

The Legion Compound commander exhaled a sigh of relief as he watched the prison bus drive past his office on the way to the fuel dock. He, however, would not be fully satisfied until the mystery of where the bus had been and the reason for its delay was explained. He pressed the intercom button on his desk.

"Bring me the bus driver with his logbook."

Word of the bulkhead door failure and the foul stench emitting from the bus had reached the assistant within minutes of the bus's arrival at the gate.

"Sir, there has been an environmental protection system failure in the bus. May I suggest…"

The commander's voice boomed over the intercom. "Get me the damn driver and his stinking logbook."

"Yes, sir. Right away, sir."

The assistant chuckled to himself at the irony of the commander's demand for the "stinking logbook."

Chet followed the troop carrier to the fuel dock where two awaiting Enforcers guided him to a location between a row of steel cages on the right and a fuel pump island on the left. Memories of being at the same fuel dock with his big rig and Ruby hidden in the OHO trailer weighed on his heart. The three months that had past seemed like years and the man he was then seemed a stranger.

He leaned back and spoke as softly as the suit's voice system would permit.

"You need to come up here when I get out. Stay in the cab if you can."

Bruce pushed the bulkhead door open a few inches.

"Gladly. It's real nasty lookin' back here. Thank God I can't smell what I see. I dosed the head bags. They'll be out of it a while."

One of the fuel dock Enforcers banged his fist on the bus door. Chet pushed the door actuator. The Enforcer stood at the door with his face mask closed. Chet saw his ID tag, M-9, and wondered if they were of the same rank.

"Commander wants you at his office with the logbook."

Chet reached into the document pocket attached to the driver's seat and pulled out the logbook.

"He wants you fueled, loaded, and out of here. So, get to it."

Chet resisted questioning the "loaded" part of the order and got his answer when he saw the occupied cages lined up next to the bus. He stepped out of the bus with the logbook tucked under his left arm.

"Point me to the commander's office."

The Enforcer raised his gloved hand and pointed to a prefabricated, green metal structure that Chet recognized from the last time they had the misfortune of being in the Legion Compound.

Chet glanced back into the cab and saw Bruce sitting in the driver's seat.

"T-12, stay in bus and watch the prisoners till I get back."

Bruce had seen the Enforcer's method of saluting and acknowledged the order without speaking by crossing his right arm and closed fist over his chest.

*****

The staff assistant tapped on the partially open door to the commander's office. The commander barked an order in response, "Come!"

The assistant marched the short distance to the commander's desk and stood at attention awaiting permission to speak.

"Where is the driver?"

"He is walking this way as we speak, sir. May I suggest that you meet with him outside?"

The commander looked up and made eye contact with the assistant for the first time since he entered the room.

"And, pray tell, why should I do that?"

There was a knock on the door before the assistant could answer. The commander and the assistant looked toward the door and saw Enforcer T-9 standing in the open doorway with his helmet on and facemask opened. Chet took the prayerful risk that neither man had ever met Enforcer T-9 before. He remained in the doorway with the logbook held in his left hand.

"Sir, this is the driver of the prison bus."

Chet nodded in acknowledgment. A gentle breeze flowed through the open doorway into the office carrying with it the stench of the bus that clung to Chet's suit. The assistant held his hand over his nose and mouth. His words were spoken as someone who was about to vomit.

"Sir, am I dismissed?"

The commander stood and pointed to the door. "Both of you get out of my office and close the door behind you."

The assistant asked, "Sir, what about the logbook?"

He remained standing and continued pointing at the door. "Copy the logbook and get him and the prisoners the hell off my post."

"Sir. Yes, sir."

Chet waited for the assistant to close the door and handed him the logbook. "Here you go. How long before we can go? We're behind schedule."

The assistant slipped on rubber gloves and grasped the logbook with his fingertips. "Go to the bus and help with the loading. I will bring the logbook. Here, take these fuel cards and go!"

Chet did not know whether to salute or just turn and leave. When the assistant turned toward the copy machine, Chet turned and left.

As Chet walked back to the bus, he watched the last of the three occupied cages being rolled into the rear door and onto the bus's overhead rail system. Then he noticed Bruce and one of the Fuel Depot Enforcers standing face-to-face behind the bus having what appeared to be a heated exchange. As he got closer, he called out, "What the hell's goin' on here!"

The Fuel Depot Enforcer stepped back and turned to face Chet as he approached.

"You people aren't dumping that stinkin' body bag here. It's your problem."

Chet handed the Fuel Depot Enforcer the fuel cards then turned to Bruce and pointed toward the bus.

"Get your ass back in the bus. We're pullin' out as soon I get the logbooks."

The Fuel Dock Enforcer mumbled as he walked away, "Yeah, get your ass back in the bus."

Bruce and Chet walked to the bus together and Bruce whispered, "Nicely done."

CHAPTER 49

East of Legion Compound, Gallup, NM

Chet suspected but Bruce was unaware that they were without Angelic support from the time the escort vehicles merged with them west of the Legion Compound until the bus was well clear of the east gate. Had the Angels of Light been with them, the massive gathering of Dark Angels at the Compound would have scattered and threatened the surrounding community of Gallup.

Chet felt the return of the Angels of Light surrounding the bus as he drove west toward Albuquerque.

"They're back."

"Who's back?"

Chet held up his right hand and made a circling motion.

"Our Guardians."

Bruce looked out the window and then back at Chet.

"You mean those Angels that gagged me at our meeting with Ruby and Lewis?"

Chet chuckled, "Yup."

"How do you know? You seein' them like Ruby said she did?"

Chet shook his head and tapped his chest. "No, can't see them. I just know they're here."

"So, you're sayin' we didn't have God helpin' back there?"

"Not sayin' that. I just know that they left and now they're back."

"Glad you know what's goin' on. I still don't get it."

Chet reached over and patted him on the left shoulder. "Yeah you do. You heard what Ruby and Captain Lewis said about our job. Help, save, and protect folks like those in the back."

167

Bruce nodded in agreement. "When can we pull over and clean it up back there?"

Chet pointed to an exit ahead. "How about we pull over down there?"

Bruce tapped his seat. "Kill the tracker?"

"No, we can leave it on if we only stop for ten or fifteen minutes."

"Let's do it."

Chet slowed and took the exit that led to a frontage road along the edge of a deep, dry gully. He pulled over onto the gravel shoulder and when he opened the bus door, a cool breeze laden with the scent of sage and desert flora drifted into the cab. The fresh natural scent caused both men to breathe deeply.

Bruce reached for the latch to open the bulkhead door.

"Masks down."

Before closing his face mask, Chet responded, "I'll get the rear doors. We gotta make this quick."

Bruce nodded in agreement.

When both front and rear doors were opened, the fresh desert breeze flushed the rank air out of the prison chamber. The young men in the cages crept back against their cage walls in fear of what was happening. Chet stood behind Bruce as he uncoiled the wall mounted wash-down hose and hit the pump switch with his fist. He directed the spray from the nozzle onto the floor under the cages and pushed the sewage out the rear of the bus.

Bruce moved toward the rear as he worked and when he was past the cage containing the body bag, Chet opened the cage door and zipped the bag closed. He then opened the cages of the Enforcer and Jud and pulled off their head coverings. Both men remained unconscious and lying on their cage floors.

As Bruce reached the rear of the bus, he called out to Chet, "Kill the pump."

They opened their face masks, and Bruce joined Chet at the cages of the young men who were kneeling in the cages with their hands covering their genitals.

Chet spoke first. "You're safe. We're not going to harm you."

The men looked at both Chet and Bruce with puzzled faces mixed with fear.

Bruce spoke next. "We stole the bus and you're safe with us." He turned to Chet. "What now?"

"We get the body bag off the bus and hit the road."

Bruce addressed the men, "Sorry, guys. You gotta stay in there a while longer."

None of the men spoke as Chet and Bruce walked away. It would take some time for them to recover from the trauma and understand what was happening.

Chet opened the cage holding the body bag and pulled one end out of the opening. Bruce grabbed the other end and they carried the bag to the dry gully.

They swung the bag back and forth a few times and Chet shouted, "Now!"

The bag tumbled down into the gulch and burst open on final impact spewing fluids and the smell of death onto the sandy desert floor.

Chet turned away and gagged. "Let's get outta here."

CHAPTER 50

Interstate 40 Near Grants, NM

Bruce's voice echoed from the back of the bus. "I found a tarp back here. Canvas."

Chet answered from the cab, "That could work."

Bruce pulled the olive-drab-colored tarp from a net bag hanging on the bulkhead wall next to the wash-down hose. He tossed it onto the floor and unfolded it while bracing himself from the swaying motion of the moving bus. By using his outstretched arm to measure, he cut the tarp into two large sections. Once satisfied with the measurements, he refolded the tarp and cut the sections into four equal sized squares. He then made one straight line cut in the center of each piece.

The three young men in their cages watched and wondered as Bruce gathered up the pieces of canvas and walked toward them. He opened the cage doors and handed one to each man.

"Pull these on like you would a poncho."

The young men hurriedly draped the canvas pieces over their naked bodies and pushed their heads through the straight cuts in the center.

Bruce watched to see if the makeshift clothing worked and smiled warmly when the young men all looked back at him and returned his smile with their dirt-smeared faces.

"You can get outta there if you want."

To his surprise, all three remained in their cages curled up in their new ponchos. He walked forward to Jud's cage, reached his arm through the bars, and grasped Jud's ankle.

"You up yet?"

Jud grumbled an unintelligible response.

"Jud's wakin' up."

Chet answered, "What about the other?"

"Don't know yet."

Bruce used more caution with the Enforcer than he had with Jud. He pulled a short length of wash-down hose from the rack, aimed the nozzle, and hit the switch. The spray hit the Enforcer in the face and forced his head back against the cage wall. No visible response. He called out to Chet.

"Not sure if he's alive or not. What do you think?"

"Leave him and come up here. We've got company."

Bruce quickly moved forward and slipped into the passenger seat.

Chet pointed to the outside mirror on Bruce's side. "See it?"

Bruce studied he image in the mirror and saw a gray bus following them about three quarters of a mile back. "Could be another prison bus."

Chet's mind began to fill with information he could not have humanly known. "No, it's a Capitia Officials bus."

Bruce turned to him with a look of disbelief. "How can you tell?"

Chet glanced in the mirror and answered, "I just know."

"But I don't see anything that makes it different than this bus."

"I don't either. I just know."

Bruce shook his head. "Okay, so what do we do?"

"We're gonna just keep rollin' and you're gonna sit shotgun till it's gone."

Chet reached out his hand toward Bruce. "Grab hold. We're gonna pray."

Bruce gripped Chet's outstretched hand and bowed his head.

Chet scanned the mirror and road ahead as he prayed. "Lord, we need some help. I know who they are and I know what they want."

He released Bruce's hand and looked in the mirror just in time to see the bus swerve to the left and explode into a ball of fire. Bruce heard the explosion, raised his head, and looked in the passenger side mirror.

"My god! What just happened?"

Chet's answer was a soft whisper that Bruce barely heard and struggled to understand. "The power of God just happened."

Chet and Bruce were not aware of the roadblock that awaited them over the next rise. Nor did they know what caused the fiery destruction of the threat behind them.

Chet took a deep breath and exhaled a sigh of relief as they pulled further away from the smoking rubble of what had been a Capitia bus loaded with Enforcers. However, his relief was short-lived as they crested the next rise. Before them was a barricade of fallen trees lying across the highway and four mud-covered pickup trucks parked along the grassy shoulders on both sides of the road.

Chet began to slow their approach speed and made a hand signal to Bruce to lower their face masks. The men had played around with the suits systems and voice commands enough to use the basic self-defense tools in the suits.

Chet's modulated voice carried through the suits intercom system to Bruce. "Not sure what this is, but I'm seein' dirty pickups."

Bruce responded, "No Enforcers, either."

Chet rolled the bus to a stop about twenty yards from the log-pile barrier. They sat in silence for a few minutes, minutes that seemed like an hour.

As they sat scanning the area ahead of the bus, they noticed that the roadblock appeared to be unmanned. Both Chet and Bruce then saw motion in their respective outside mirrors. Men dressed in dirty camo and carrying rifles and shotguns, unlike that of the Redeemers Clan, approached single file from the rear hugging close to the bus body. Chet's first reaction was to accelerate forward, but it was obvious that they would not get far before hitting the log barrier.

Chet opened his face mask and tapped Bruce on the helmet. "Let's pop our helmets off. These guys need to know who we are."

Bruce opened his face mask and reached back to release the helmet. "We need to know who the hell they are. Could be another clan."

Chet's response was to remove his helmet and press the lever that opened the bus door. Bruce turned in his seat and stepped out through the open door. He turned and faced the approaching men on his side. Chet followed quickly and stood behind Bruce facing forward. Bruce watched the men approached from the rear, and Chet watched as more men came around from the front of the bus.

The man closest to Chet raised his right hand in a halt signal and both groups of men stopped in their tracks with weapons at the ready.

The man who deployed the hand signal asked Chet a question that confirmed Chet's and Bruce's new names and calling.

"Are you Melek and Gibbor from the Redeemers Clan?"

Chet was quick to answer. Not out of fear, but because he had accepted and embraced his new and powerful identity. "Yes, and you are…?"

The man lowered his rifle and the others followed. "I am Captain Scott, leader of the Freedom Clan. We have been expecting you. Welcome."

Chet gestured toward the bus. "We have passengers in there. Okay to bring 'em out?"

Captain Scott nodded in the affirmative.

Chet turned to Bruce. "Bring 'em out but leave Jud caged."

CHAPTER 51

Legion Compound, Gallup, NM

A missing busload of Capitia Enforcers and two suits gone rogue. Both spell disgrace and death to the commander of the Gallup Legion Compound. He stormed across the compound, burst into the Control Room, and demanded everyone's attention.

"Which of you is responsible for tracking vehicles?"

The six technicians turned away from their monitors and immediately stood at attention. None of them spoke for what seemed like an eternity to the commander. The only sound in the room was the harmonic hum of the electronic equipment and the commander's heavy breathing.

His anger grew as evidenced by the intensity in his voice.

"I said, who is responsible for tracking vehicles?!"

A young technician to his right raised his hand and answered in a tone of frightened submission, "Sir, I do, sir."

The commander turned and marched toward the young man. The stomping sound of his boots slamming the floor echoed through the room. The other five technicians immediately turned and busied themselves at their work stations.

The commander pointed at the technician's chair and abruptly ordered him to sit.

"I have received a report from this station that you have lost contact with the vehicle carrying a squad of Enforcers. Is that true?"

The young technician's voice trembled as he answered, "Sir, yes, sir."

The commander slammed his hands on the desk. "Stop that!"

"Yes, sir."

"How is it possible to lose an entire bus?"

The technician moved slightly away from the commander before answering. "Destroyed or disabled, sir."

"What do you mean by that?"

He regained enough composure to respond without trembling. "The only way we can permanently lose the ability to track is if the vehicle is destroyed or if the tracking feature is disabled."

The commander then turned facing the other work stations and spoke in a slightly calmer voice, "Who is responsible for tracking suits?"

An older woman across the room raised her hand. "I am, sir."

"Come here," he ordered.

She walked briskly across the room and stopped a few feet away from the commander. Her posture was at full attention with her arms at her side and hands clenched.

"How is it possible to lose the ability to track a suit?"

"Sir, it would require disabling of the tracking function or if the self-destruct feature was initiated."

He leaned back slightly as if the force of an idea had pressed against his forehead. "Self-destruct feature? Tell me more."

WE GOT THE OLD MAN THINKIN' NOW.
CHECK WITH THE BOSS.
OH, HELL NO!

His words caused her to gasp and briefly place her right hand over her mouth. "Sir. I am so sorry, I thought—"

The commander cut her off mid-sentence. "You thought what?!"

She immediately snapped back to attention. "Sir, I assumed that you had Security Standing for that information. Please forgive me."

"How dare you question my Standing. Continue!"

"Yes, sir. The suits are individually wired to receive and respond to unique radio signals for communication and monitoring. Each suit has a call frequency and the tracking feature simply bounces the signal back to us."

The commander raised his left hand to his chin, glanced at the ceiling, then locked his eyes onto hers.

"Take me to your workstation."

CHAPTER 52

Freedom Clan, NM

Chet and Bruce had retrieved the map case and Bruce's gear from the bus and changed into civilian clothes given to them by the Freedom Clan.

The Enforcers' suits and helmets lay on the ground nearby. Jud had been brought out and was sitting on the step of the bus as ordered by Chet.

The sound of a galloping horse approaching from the direction of the smoldering bus wreck caught the men's attention. Captain Scott stepped away from the group and stood facing the incoming rider.

The young rider shouted to Captain Scott before bringing his steed to a halt, "Sir, there is a drone flying around the bus we killed."

Chet, Bruce, and Jud watched and listened.

Captain Scott approached the horse and stroked its panting neck as he spoke. "You want to kill it?"

"Yes, sir!"

Captain Scott tapped the stock of the rifle in the saddle holster. "You need a scope?"

The young rider answered with a tone of absolute confidence, "No, sir!"

Captain Scott stepped back before he spoke. "Then get to it!"

The young rider pulled the reigns hard to the left and shouted over his shoulder as the horse bolted away. "Yes, sir!"

The urgency of the situation could be heard in Captain Scott's voice. "This bus needs to be gone…now!"

Chet, Bruce, and Jud were unaware of the two clansmen lying under the bus, draining diesel fuel into a plastic container. They had been instructed to leave only ten gallons of fuel in the tank.

Captain Scott scanned the gathering and asked, "Volunteers?"

To Chet and Bruce's surprise, Jud raised his hand, stood up, and spoke, "Me, I'll do it."

Captain Scott looked toward Chet for a response. Chet turned to Bruce. "Want do ya think?"

Bruce was quick to answer. "Works for me."

Chet turned toward Captain Scott to answer, but Jud interrupted. "I'll do it if you give me one of them suits."

After a brief discussion between Chet and Captain Scott, it was decided that Jud would get a suit but not a helmet. Jud reacted to the limitation with childlike body language and a whiney tone in his voice. "Come on, that's not right."

Chet's response was quick. "Your choice. Go without the helmet or stay here and get what's comin' to ya."

The report of a single rifle shot caused the men to look in the direction the young rider had gone.

Captain Scott immediately picked up one of the suits and tossed it on the ground at Jud's feet. "Drone's dead. You going or not?"

Jud stood staring at the suit as if expecting it to address him. The lack of response prompted Captain Scott to turn and point to one of the clansmen near him.

"Get that bus out of here."

The clansman began to walk toward the bus when Jud spoke up. "Okay, okay!"

Bruce assisted him as he stepped into the boots and pulled the suit up to his shoulders. It hung on his scrawny frame like a wrinkled, black deflated balloon.

Chet pointed toward the bus door. "Go before I change my mind. Don't stop and don't come back."

Jud picked up his backpack and waddled to the bus. The saggy weight of the suit and the backpack draped over his left arm caused him to struggle as he climbed into the driver's seat. A few minutes later the rumbling sound of the bus engine starting and the grinding of gears announced his departure.

He pulled away and passed the logs that had lain across the road. At that moment he felt the same feeling of escape and victory as he had riding in the back of the prison trash truck when it passed the gate and guard tower.

However, his elation was short-lived. For some reason the boots began to heat up and burn the bottoms of his feet. The intensity increased until the pain shooting up his legs caused him to pass out and fall forward onto the steering wheel.

At that same moment the suit and both helmets on the ground near the clansmen began to smolder and melt. The men stood back and watched as the fusion reactors in the boots overheated and imploded taking the entire suit with it. At the same time both helmets dissolved as the acid encased lining burst open.

HE'S DONE.

YA…WELL DONE.

LET'S GET OUT OF HERE.

WHY?

LOOK AROUND, STUPID.

What the Dark Angels saw and feared were the six Angels of Light watching them from above the Freedom Clan camp.

*****

Meanwhile, at the Gallup Legion Checkpoint, the commander asked the suit technician, "Is it done?"

She paused before answering, which irritated the commander to the point of a measured, explosive response. "IS. IT. DONE?!"

She answered with a trembling voice, "Sir, without confirmation I can't be sure."

She continued, "We have never deployed the self-destruct feature in real time, only in testing when the suits were designed."

The commander turned and marched toward the door. He shouted back at her as he walked away. "It's about time. Don't you think?!"

CHAPTER 53

Freedom Clan, NM

The Freedom Clan was made up of men and only men. Each wore military camo fatigues, military boots, and covered their heads with black skull caps like that of a motorcycle gang. Bruce recognized the various color schemes of the fatigues. Some were blue/gray like Air Force and Navy and others were brown/tan like Army and Marines.

As they followed Captain Scott through the camp, they saw that there were no tents or above-ground structures, only foxholes covered with pine branches and leaves.

Captain Scott led them to a wooded area beyond the camp. They stopped in a small clearing where a long lean-to shelter had been constructed of fallen trees and roofed with pine branches. Several horses grazed in the clearing and others were closed in stalls in the lean-to.

Captain Scott gestured to a nearby fire pit surrounded by logs cut flat as benches. The three men sat on the log benches and Captain Scott opened the conversation.

"I've got questions and I know you do. You go first."

Chet leaned forward slightly and asked the questions that he and Bruce had pondered. "How do you know about us and how much do you know?"

Captain Scott smiled, nodded toward the horses, and answered, "We saw you with the Redeemers Clan then you took out the bus on Highway 40. Captain Lewis had told me it was going to happen and I had our rider stop and watch on his way to Flagstaff."

Bruce looked at Chet before speaking. "Captain Lewis?"

"Yes."

Bruce had a puzzled look on his face as he continued. "How did you get that information from Captain Lewis?"

Captain Scott raised both his hands as if surrendering as he began to answer. "Let me answer that and the other questions I know you have."

Then he began to explain. "We and the Redeemers Clan are not the only ones. So far, we have found two others. The Cave Clan in the lava tube caves northwest of Flagstaff and the Mesa Clan beyond Sedona."

He paused to give them time to process the new information and then continued. "We carry messages and news to and from the clans we have found so far. We do it on horseback at night. We keep knowledge of our mission limited to only the Melek and Gibbor of each clan. It was Captain Lewis who messaged us that you were coming by. He also warned us that you may be pursued by Capitia."

Bruce asked the next question, "So, it was you that took out that bus?"

"We were ready, and yes we did."

Bruce shook his head. "That thing exploded. What did you use?"

Captain Scott knew there were more important matters to discuss and gave a brief answer, "We have an armory. Now I need to know more about your mission."

Chet reached into his map case and pulled out his charts. "There is a place in Albuquerque we need to find."

Captain Scott pointed at the charts. "You know Albuquerque is pure hell, right?"

Bruce answered, "Explain."

"Beheadings. That's one of the locations where it happens. They do it on what's called Judgment Day."

Chet responded, "I knew. Those young men we brought here in the bus were heading there.

Captain Scott noticed the airline logo on Chet's map case and changed the subject. "You a pilot?"

"Was, why?"

Captain Scott stood and gestured toward the lean-to. "I think I know how you can get to Albuquerque. Come with me."

They walked the short distance to the lean-to where Captain Scott stopped at a stall holding two horses: a dark mare and her twenty-month old yearling.

"There's an airpark southwest of here off Highway 260. Enforcers don't patrol there much, and I know for a fact that some of the homes have planes in the hangars."

A deep involuntary breath filled Chet's chest. "Tell me more."

The mare stepped closer to the men and pressed her nose against Captain Scott's shoulder.

"This girl can take you there and find her way back. The yearling will follow."

He paused long enough for Chet and Bruce to consider the idea and then continued. "We'll outfit you with everything you need to get to the airpark. After that you're on your own."

Two Angels of Light watching and listening from above the lean-to received their orders.

GO AND PREPARE A WAY FOR THEM.

YES, LORD.

CHAPTER 54

Redeemers Clan, AZ

The heavy thumping of helicopter blades slicing through the air caused all eyes to look in the direction of the ominous sound.

Lieutenant Marks was first to hear and first to take action. He immediately ran to a pickup truck parked under the tree near the north lookout and drove through the camp warning and directing the clan. The evacuation plan had only been done as drills, but this time it looked real.

Captain Lewis had also heard the incoming threat and was at the beach by the hospital tent helping load a raft with medical supplies. Fortunately, there were no bedridden patients.

The clan members followed the evacuation procedure to the letter and within minutes were entering the knee-deep water of the creek each carrying their individual evacuation supplies. They lined up in pairs and moved quickly south and away from the approaching threat. Lieutenant Marks led the way followed by three men and Ruby pushing the supply raft through the water.

Captain Lewis waited on the beach and watched as his precious clan pushed through the shallow water and away from the only security they had known since The Vanishing. Soon everyone had passed the first bend in the creek and was out of sight, hidden by the dense forests that had sheltered and protected them. He stood on the beach and made one last scan of the abandoned camp before wading into the creek. The sound of the helicopter stopped, which caused Captain Lewis to move to the edge of the creek and squat down in the water behind an outcropping bolder.

One Angel of Light went with the clan and the other stayed behind with Captain Lewis. A familiar feeling of security and spiritual power poured over him, confirming the Angel's presence.

He took a deep breath and whispered, "Thank you, Father."

CHAPTER 55

Freedom Clan, NM

The morning sun burned down onto the clearing as the men prepared for the horseback ride to the airpark. Chet opened the chart and spread it over the saddle. The mare held stone still for him. Captain Scott studied the chart and, after a few minutes, tapped his index finger onto the location of the airpark. Chet looked closely and saw the faint icon he recognized as a private landing strip.

"How long to get there?"

"It's about a hundred and fifty miles. The mare trots around six miles per hour. You should get there in about a day of steady riding. Leave now and you should get there by morning."

Chet folded the chart, slipped it into his saddlebag, and handed his map case to Captain Scott. "Keep this for me?"

"No problem."

Chet did not realize he had left his cell phone and solar charger in the map case.

Bruce and Captain Scott's lieutenant stood near the yearling loading saddle bags the mare would carry. Bruce and the saddle would be the only loads the young horse would bear. The lieutenant helped Bruce slip on a nylon shoulder holster modified to carry two pistols and four clips. Then he handed Bruce a Glock 9mm that exactly matched the one he carried. After confirming that the clips were full, he palmed them into the pistol grips and slipped the pistols into the holster. The lieutenant handed him two small, flat packages containing tightly folded solar blankets.

Bruce nodded his understanding of what they were for. The lieutenant smiled and walked away.

Chet mounted the mare and looked toward Bruce. "Let's do this."

Captain Scott leaned closer to Chet and the mare shifted her weight as if making it easier for Chet to hear. "I too was Melek without a clan for a time. Godspeed."

CHAPTER 56

Airstrip Heber, AZ

The horses were sure-footed and quiet but for the sound of leather rubbing leather as they made their way down the slope of a trench running parallel to the runway. The sun was rising above the treetops creating long shadows across the pine needle-covered ground, which allowed the men to scout the area relatively stealth. They walked the horses and scanned the homes in hopes of finding one of the airplanes Captain Scott had assured them were there. As they neared the house and hangar closest to the runway threshold, a bullet ricocheted off the ground less than five feet from the horses. Both horses lurched to the right, and had the men not been holding the bridles, they may have bolted away. Both men hit the ground and lay as still as possible.

Bruce pointed toward the hangar of the home they had approached. Chet immediately stood to his feet next to the mare and held both hands in the air. Bruce grumbled something unintelligible and stood up beside him. Chet slowly reached into the saddle bag and pulled out the black Bible. Bruce watched and held his breath expecting a second shot to be fired, but this time it would not be a warning. Chet began walking toward the hangar with both hands in the air. He held the Bible in his right hand with the cover facing the hangar. Bruce heard it first.

"Sounds like a woman crying."

Chet nodded his head, lowered his hands, and passed the Bible to Bruce. They continued to walk toward the hangar with the horses in tow. When Chet was close enough to be heard, he spoke out with calm authority. "We have been sent to help you."

The weeping stopped and the hangar door rolled open a few feet.

Bruce tied the horse's reins to a small tree next to the hangar and joined Chet. He had not pulled his pistols from their holsters and did not intend to. The danger they just experienced and Chet's actions had been a teaching lesson for him. He was beginning to understand, Chet is Melek, he is Gibbor.

CHAPTER 57

Albuquerque, NM

The tarmac at Albuquerque International Airport was awash with chaotic activity. Heavy equipment was placing steel barriers and bleachers into a three-quarter circle with large refrigerated box trailers positioned to complete the enclosure. The box trailers were all white with twenty-four-inch-high yellow letters, OHO, on each side.

When viewed from above, the enclosure eerily resembled the arenas of the Rome Empire where men fought to the death and Christians were devoured by wild animals as entertainment for the masses. Large mobile devices designed to efficiently decapitate and preserve human remains stood in the center of the arena.

As the arena was being assembled, Enforcers were preparing to surround the city and gather people into buses to be transported to the Judgment Day event. Those who had declared loyalty to Capitia would be loaded onto buses bound for the bleachers. All others would be captured and taken to the Loyalty Center at the airport terminal for processing.

A large black tent was constructed outside the arena near the refrigerated box trailers. Black was chosen to create the highest interior ambient temperature for two reasons; to create high body-core temperature of the occupants and cause maximum discomfort. The tents where occupied by those who had been captured in the surrounding areas and transported to Albuquerque for Judgment Day. Had the Redeemers Clan not hijacked the bus near Winslow, its cargo would have been in the tent.

Chapter 58

Airstrip Heber, AZ

The hangar looked exactly like a hangar should, clean, organized, and well lighted. In the center, like a trophy in a case, stood a stark white Diamond DA42, twin engine, four-place aircraft.

It all looked normal until they saw the corpse lying on the floor next to the aircraft's right baggage compartment. The woman led them to the body and dropped to her knees weeping.

"He was getting us ready to leave. I thought he dropped one of the suitcases."

She leaned over and brushed her hand over his bald scalp. "Then I looked and saw him, here."

Bruce bent down, studied the man's eyes, and felt his neck and limbs. He stood up and whispered to Chet, "He's been dead around six hours.

Chet nodded toward the hangar door as he spoke, "I'll handle this… you take watch."

Bruce nodded and moved to the open hangar door.

Chet bent down next to the woman and helped her stand up. They walked to two chairs along the hangar wall where she sat down and Chet knelt in front of her. He spoke in a gentle voice just above a whisper. "We will take care of you and we will get you to safety."

She looked up and wiped a tear from her cheek with the back of her hand. "Safety?"

"Yes, but you need to trust us."

She paused before responding and spoke with absolute submission in her voice, "Okay."

Chet took the woman's hands into his. "Thank you."

She looked toward the body of her dead husband. "Can you bury him for me, please?'

"Of course. Now listen very carefully."

"Okay."

Chet rose, sat in the chair next to her, and pointed to the airplane. "We need your permission to use your plane."

She answered without hesitation, "Yes, of course, but can you tell me how you will get me to safety?"

"Yes, but you must be brave."

"Okay."

Chet walked her to the hangar door and pointed to the mare. "We will get you on that horse and she will take you to some good men who will help you. It's a long ride, but you will be safe."

"How?"

Chet smiled softly as he spoke, "She knows the way home."

CHAPTER 59

Freedom Clan, NM

The exhausted rider dismounted and handed the reins over to the clansman whose duty it was to care for the horses. He had made it back to camp before sunrise as Captain Scott expects, but he dreaded the debriefing to come. He pulled his rifle from the saddle holster and tossed his saddle bags over his shoulder. And as he always did after a mission, he leaned his forehead against the horse's warm damp neck and whispered, "Thank you."

Captain Scott had been watching and waiting for the rider's return as he did each morning. Often the news was encouraging and sometimes it carried more emotional weight than any caring man could handle. This was one of those mornings.

The rider saw Captain Scott sitting on a log bench at the fire pit and joined him there.

Captain Scott spoke first. "Welcome back, soldier."

The rider leaned his rifle against the log, tossed his saddle bags onto the pine needle-covered ground, and sat down. His face and hands were cover in dust that clung to him like wet paint and a bead of sweat dripped from under his black skull cap onto the ground.

"Hard ride?"

"Yes, sir."

"Tell me about it when you're ready."

Those words released the pain he carried causing him to sigh deeply as a tear rolled down his smudged cheek.

"They're gone, sir."

Captain Scott patiently waited for him to continue.

"The Redeemers Clan is gone. I took a chance and rode into Winslow to find Red Cap."

The rider wiped his eyes and nose with his sleeve and continued. "He said he saw the women from the clan getting loaded onto a bus on the edge of town. No men, just women."

Captain Scott breathed deeply and said, "Breeders."

Hearing that, the rider's demeanor changed from grief to anger. He stood up and picked up his rifle. "We've got to fix this, sir."

All that Captain Scott could do or say was, "I know, son. God, how I know."

CHAPTER 60

Airstrip, White Mountains, AZ

"This is one good lookin' bird."

Chet ran his hands up and down the leading edges of the left engine's three-blade propeller.

"Yup, she is."

They had buried the woman's husband and watched the morning mist envelope the woman as the mare carried her away with the yearling obediently following. She had agreed to give them the airplane and kissed them on the cheek before mounting the mare. The warmth of her gratitude could be felt in the kisses.

Chet finished the preflight inspection and climbed into the cockpit. It felt good to be in the left seat again. He found a laminated card in the side pocket and located the POH, Pilot's Operating Handbook. The two-sided laminated card had everything he needed to know about the plane's performance and operating speeds. Bruce stood by the right wing and watched Chet familiarize himself with the controls and instrument panel.

"This what you used to fly?"

"Close enough. Roll back the door and climb in."

When the door was fully open, Chet started the left engine and signaled Bruce to climb aboard. The plane could be flown from either of the front seats as evidenced by the joysticks projecting up from the center knee position of the seats.

Bruce tapped the joystick between his legs and let out a nervous chuckle. "Feel like I'm sitting in a fighter jet."

Chet nodded and looked at him with a mischievous smile. "We're flyin' at treetop level…full throttle. Should see around 200 knots."

He then reached up, pulled the canopy down, and started the right engine. The taxi from the hangar to the runway threshold was less the one hundred feet, and Chet did not hesitate to throttle up as soon the nose was pointed down the runway centerline. The air was cool, which was the perfect condition for an aggressive climb-out. They were well above the tallest trees in less than a minute and Chet banked hard to the left, settling in on a compass heading for Albuquerque.

He still did not realize he had left his phone in the map case back at the Freedom Clan.

The Angels of Light watched the plane bank away to the northeast.

PREPARE FOR THEIR ARRIVAL.
YES, LORD.

CHAPTER 61

Albuquerque, NM

The entire city of Albuquerque was under siege by Enforcers who kicked down doors and shot those who resisted with tranquilizer darts. It seemed that no one could hide or escape, yet some did.

As Chet and Bruce raced toward the small black dot on Chet's chart, hundreds of Enforcers moved around the city in an ever-shrinking circle, like the tightening of a noose around the city.

The prisoners held in the black tent were being evaluated and marked for the final destination of their bodies. They all stood naked shoulder to shoulder as OHO medical technicians performed physical examinations. The depressing sounds of men and women weeping harmonically blended with the cyclical hissing sound of the hazmat suite respirators worn by the technicians.

Each prisoner was marked with a one-inch high OHO stamp across their foreheads and chests. Those who received a red stamp were herded to the left exit of the tent and each given a red robe. Those with a black stamp were taken to the right and given black robes. The robes were specifically designed for decapitation and preservation. A drawcord and Velcro flap were sewn into the neck and foot as was a hood that hung down the front just below the chin. To assure a sterile outcome, the robes were coated inside with antibacterial gel, that when touched releases a pungent scent of cinnamon overcome by ammonia.

When the execution was done, the decapitated head was captured in the hood, and the neck and foot of the robe were drawn closed and sealed by Velcro flaps. The robes effectively become sterile body bags. Red bags would be loaded into box trailers marked with yellow OHO logos for delivery to harvesting centers, and the black bags would be sent to incinerators located outside of the city limits.

Buses were arriving and the bleachers were beginning to fill as Dark Angels gathered in their midst hissing and taunting with evil glee. The moment of judgment was one last breath away for those who dare resist loyalty to Capitia.

CHAPTER 62

Southwest of Albuquerque, NM

The white twin-engine plane sped over the changing terrain that screamed past a mere seventy feet below. The forest was replaced by rolling hills and fields and further ahead the men could to see the suburbs that spread over the western outskirts of Albuquerque.

Chet tapped Bruce on the knee, pointed up with his index finger, and shouted over the din of the engines and wind noise.

"Gonna pop up and find a place to set us down."

Bruce indicated that he heard and understood by nodding his head in the affirmative.

They had flown under the radar for the past hour and fifteen minutes, and Chet assumed that when they climbed, they would pop up on the screens at Albuquerque International Airport. What he did not know was that Capitia had closed the airport and shut down the radar in order to deploy all available manpower for crowd control and to facilitate activities of Judgment Day.

The plane was moving too fast for rotation to an aggressive climb-rate prompting Chet to pull the throttles back. When the airspeed slowed to 175 knots, he eased back on the joystick and climbed to an altitude of one thousand feet in a mere forty-five seconds. At that altitude he leveled off and scanned the area ahead. In less than three seconds he rolled the plane into a spiraling dive and leveled off at two hundred feet above the ground.

Bruce shouted one word that said it all, "Whoa!"

Chet pointed to a grass field next to several homes and a large, partially collapsed building. "Grab the saddle bags and tighten your seat belt."

Bruce complied without speaking as the rooftops of the homes below grew steadily closer.

Chet pulled the throttles back to the stops causing the engines to shut down and the propellers to automatically feather. "We're goin' in dead-stick."

Chet lowered the landing gear, which helped slow the plane to one hundred knots and out of habit whispered, "Three green." When he pressed the flaps lever fully down, the airspeed decreased and the decent increased. A spot on the nearest edge of a wet grassy soccer field remained fixed in the windscreen as they silently glided toward the earth. He balanced the plane between flight and stall as evidenced by an occasional chirp of the stall warning horn.

The flair, touchdown, and rollout were perfect until the nose gear dropped into a deep divot three quarters of the way down the field. The nose gear collapsed causing the underbelly of the nose and tips of the propellers to augur into the muddy grass. The force of the deceleration threw the men forward against their shoulder harnesses.

Chet grabbed the canopy lever, pushed it open, and released his seat belt. Bruce tossed the saddle bags onto the wing and climbed out. There was so much he wanted to say, but it had to wait.

The Angels of Light were already there waiting for their arrival.

GUIDE THEM TO THE CHAMBER.

YES, LORD.

A contingent of two Enforcers was assigned to patrol the west quadrant of the city in hopes of capturing dissidents after the sweep. One of them pointed in the direction of the soccer field.

"I think I just saw a plane go down."

*****

The nearest place for Chet and Bruce to run for shelter was the partially collapsed building at the end of the soccer field. Water splashed from under their boots and soaked their pant legs as they sprinted across the field. Bruce ran with the saddle bags over his left forearm while Chet led the way to an opening in the building's rubble. As they approached the opening, Chet slowed and stopped as if there was no threat.

Bruce caught up and stopped next to him. "What's wrong?"

Chet did not speak but instead pointed at the opening they were running toward. It was in the shape of a triangle with its longest leg along the ground. When the building had collapsed, a concrete column had fallen across a broken concrete beam. The two interlocked pieces created what appeared to be a cross standing on its side...a cross down.

Chet looked at Bruce with bewilderment in eyes. "Do you see what I see?"

"Yeah, a hole to run to. Let's go!"

Chet reached for the saddle bags under Bruce's arm. "Need my phone."

"No! We need to get out of sight."

The opening was a mere twenty yards ahead. When they reached it, Bruce ducked in ahead of Chet. His voice echoed from the cavity. "All clear...get in here." Bruce had pulled a flashlight from the saddle bag, and as he scanned the space, he noticed a partially compressed metal framed structure in the far corner. He determined it to be the best defendable space available.

"Get my phone."

Bruce shone the beam of the flashlight onto the metal frame. "Not until we get back there."

Concrete dust rose in the air as they crawled deeper into the cavity on hands and knees. Chet stopped when he reached the metal frame and Bruce positioned himself between Chet and the now somewhat distant opening.

Chet held out his hand. "Phone."

Bruce pushed the saddle bags across the floor and watched Chet dump out the contents. There were several minutes of silence and rummaging before Chet realized that he had left the phone in his map case back at the Freedom Clan.

Bruce gave Chet a stop signal with his hand and placed his index finger over his lips. Chet had also heard the sounds of men talking from outside the cavity and tapping from somewhere above them.

CHAPTER 63

Freedom Clan, NM

"Excuse me, sir."

"Enter."

The clansman whose duty it was to care for the horses stepped into Captain Scott's dugout. He looked up and acknowledged the clansman's presence.

"Sir, the mare and yearling are back, and the mare has a rider."

Captain Scott stood and walked briskly toward the clansman. "Rider?"

"Yes, sir, an old woman."

The men exited the dugout and walked to the clearing with the clansman in the lead. The mare and yearling were haltered to a post outside the lean-to with their saddles and horse blankets hung over the railing.

"Over there, sir."

Captain Scott looked inside the closest stall and saw the woman sitting in the corner on a bale of hay. He estimated her age to be around sixty, and by the looks of her clothes, shoes, and small suitcase on her lap, he assumed she had been a woman of means. He stood at the entrance of the stall with the sun to his back.

The visual effect of his dark silhouette surrounded by the bright light flooding through the opening caused here to stand, gasp, and place both hands over her mouth. Her suitcase tumbled onto the straw-covered floor.

Captain Scott saw her fear and raised his hands with palms toward her. "Don't be afraid. My name is Captain Scott."

She remained standing with her hands over her mount and staring at the suitcase at her feet.

"May I ask how you came to be here?"

Her trembling words matched the expression of fear on her face. "Two men helped me. They put me on the horse and said it would take me to safety."

She remained frozen in place as she waited to him to response.

"I see. Can you tell me who those men were?"

"Yes."

Captain Scott stepped inside the stall and stopped just arm's length away. She leaned back as he approached but managed to remain standing.

"You are safe here. Can you tell me who those men were?"

The gentle expression of compassion on Captain Scott's face and his nonthreatening body language allowed her answer in a more natural, calm voice, just above a whisper. "I only know one. He said his name was Captain Rawlins. I don't know the other man's name."

She did not understand why Captain Scott smiled as he took her hand and asked her to sit with him. "Did you help Captain Rawlins and the other man?"

"Yes, and they helped me."

Captain Scott nodded his head and waited for her to continue.

"They buried my husband. He had a heart attack or something just before the men arrived. I shot at them once, but I could tell they were not afraid, and they told me the horse knew the way home."

"How did you help them?"

Her demeanor had calmed as the feeling of relative safety radiated from Captain Scott's presence. "I gave them my husband's airplane. They said their mission was to take it to Albuquerque."

CHAPTER 64

Redeemers Clan, AZ

The ominous silence of the forest hushed all hope of survivors. The only evidence that the Redeemers Clan had once existed were the scars in the forest floor where deep tire tracks of heavy equipment had carved the soft ground in chaotic patterns. Near the creek where the hospital tent once stood was a swollen mound of raw earth that served as a mass grave.

All of the girls and women of child-bearing age were rounded up and loaded into troop trucks. The same trucks that had delivered the Enforcers to the site.

Soil erosion along the dirt road leading from Winslow to the Redeemers Clan camp had provided Legion with what they needed to find the dissidents who had hijacked buses and stolen human cargo. Rain and wind had eroded the soil and exposed sections of the wire along the dirt road.

A camera drone was deployed to descended from above the barn and flew south at twenty feet above the partially unearthed wire. When it was one hundred yards away from the barn, it was called back to the Mobile Drone Unit parked on the interstate overpass that led to the truck stop. No one in the truck stop was aware of the breech.

Lieutenant Marks was unaware of the Legion drone hovering above the wire when he tapped out a brief message. The drone had been equipped with high frequency sensors that picked up the Morse code pulses traveling through the once buried wire.

Legion trucks and equipment were dispatched and within two hours scouts were following the wire south with a fifty-troop contingent behind them. The commander of the Gallup Legion Compound watched from the safety of his helicopter as the troops crept through scrub brush like hungry beasts of prey.

Chapter 65

Bruce handed Chet the flashlight and used a hand signal instructing him to stay put. He rotated onto his hands and knees and cautiously crept toward the triangular opening they had just run though. The outside voices became more distinct as he reached the opening. He slipped his Ka-Bar knife from the belt sheath and slowly moved the blade into position. The polished blade worked as a small mirror allowing him to see the images of two Enforcers standing by the nose of the disabled plane. One of the Enforcers tapped his helmet and began making up and down, followed by left-right motions of his head.

Bruce quickly slipped the knife back into the sheath and crawled back to Chet. He placed his mouth so close to Chet's ear he could feel the heat of Bruce's breath as he whispered, "Infrared scan…lay flat."

Chet moved from his squatting positing to lie face down on the gritty floor. He turned his head away from Bruce and toward the metal frame. Bruch opened the solar blanket packs and loosely draped the solar blankets between them and where he estimated the Enforcers to be standing. Chet could not see what Bruce had done to shield their heat signature from the helmet-mounted infrared scan. But what he did see caused him to take a deep breath and touch it with his index finger. He ran his fingers over the cross shaped welded pattern on the metal frame just inches from his nose.

The sound of boots running toward them followed by shouting prompted Bruce to slip both pistols from their holsters. He lay on his belly facing the opening with both weapons at the ready just behind the blanket shield. Whoever was to pull the blanket back was in for a deadly surprise.

Then they heard the screaming. It was high pitch and likely that of a young woman.

A gravely male voice echoed through the rubble. "Got her!"

The screaming stopped and they heard a second male voice. "I'll get the truck."

Bruce remained ready to defend and waited until he heard the sound of the truck pulling away. He crawled to the opening and peered around the corner, scanning the soccer field. When he crawled back to tell Chet the Enforcers had gone, Chet spoke first. "Look at this."

Bruce knelt closer to the image. "Looks like somebody welded a cross shape on the frame."

Chet nodded and recited the last of Tom's phone message. The parts of the riddle he had not yet solved. "Col at Vai…under the cross down."

He paused and reached through the square opening of the metal frame.

"Under the cross down."

He tapped on the metal floor inside the frame and heard a distinctly hollow sound.

"Under, Bruce, under."

Bruce positioned himself closer and watched as Chet brushed away dust and debris to reveal a hinge on one side and a latch handle on the opposite side.

Chet grabbed the handle and pulled it until the panel dropped a few inches. Cool dry air rushed from the opening and carried away the fine dust from the perimeter. The hinged panel hung partially open, held in place by a counterbalance cable. Bruce pushed the panel further open intending to illuminate the space with his flashlight. As the panel reached the halfway point, lights from the cavity below suddenly came on. Both men froze and waited, expecting to hear or see something that would explain what just happened.

CHAPTER 66

Breeding Center, Phoenix, AZ

Time… What is time but the passing of things revealed and the mystery of things to come.

The stark white, sterile chamber had been designed to deprive the occupant of color, sound, and the passing of time, all for the purpose of breaking them down emotionally and spiritually.

But for Ruby it was an escape from the realities of where she was and how she had gotten there. She sat in the corner of the small cubical with her knees pulled up to her breast and her arms hugging her legs. There were no Angels of Light to soothe her, only the assurances and admonitions she had received from them as the Enforcers led her and the others to the trucks.

She knew that Captain Lewis, Lieutenant Marks, the nurses, and all who perished that day had been freed. The Angels of Light had said they were Garnered to God and she understood the admonition to heal and redeem those around her.

Soon she would be released from the cubicle and ordered to perform prenatal care, midwife duties, and care for the newborn citizens of OWO…One World Order.

CHAPTER 67

Southeast Albuquerque, NM

Battery power illuminated the light fixtures and powered the trip switch that had turned on the lights when the hatch passed the half-opened position. The subterranean chamber was stocked with jugs of water, cartons of food supplies, books, games, a Bible, and three stationary bicycles modified to charge batteries. It was obvious that someone had designed the space to house several people and children in relative comfort for an extended period of time.

Bruce stood on the steel wall-mounted ladder with his head out of the opening like that of a tank driver with his head sticking out the hatch. He felt it was a reasonably defensive position and the best hope of preventing someone from locking them into the underground chamber.

Chet walked around below looking and touching the heaps of clothing that lay on the floor. Some were horizontal as a person reclining and others were stacked as if falling off someone standing. He reached down and slowly picked up a blue denim shirt. As he lifted it off the floor, gray granular powder trickled to the floor like spilled sugar. The sight caused him to drop the shirt and step back. Immediately a phrase floated through his mind. *Ashes to ashes, dust to dust.*

His thoughts were interrupted by a warning from Bruce. "Someone's coming."

The shadows approaching the outside opening became that of three people crawling toward him on hands and knees. Bruce was not sure if they could see him in the semi-dark until the voice of a young man echoed through the space.

"Please, help us."

Before he could answer, he noticed the light from beyond becoming dimmer as the dark figures of a line of Enforcers gathered outside.

CHAPTER 68

Albuquerque, NM

The voice of the Creator of all things seen and unseen reverberated through the Heavens and over the face of the Earth.

PREPARE FOR GARNERING.

A second voice sounded with instructions to all Angels of Light. It is the voice of God's own Gibbor…Michael the Archangel.

ASSEMBLE FOR GARNERING.

The power and worldly control of Capitia had reached all of the major cities around the globe. As was decreed by Capitia, Judgment Day events would occur at high noon on the same day in every designated city. At noon in Bagdad, Iraq, the first blade dropped followed by cities in Europe and Africa as the noon hour circumvented the globe from east to west.

As noon approached in Albuquerque, Angels of Light assembled above the arena and directly above the black tent. Their presence caused the Dark Angels to flee and lurk a short distance away. The jeering of the assembled crowd decreased as the Dark Angels moved away from the arena. Soon people could be heard weeping and others begging the robed candidates to give up and embrace Capitia.

Seventy Angels of Light glided down and placed themselves around the perimeter of the arena creating an impenetrable barrier against any Dark Angel that dare interfere with the Garnering.

At exactly twelve noon, the robed victims were escorted from the tent and led single file to a staging area in clear sight of the spectators. The intensity of jeers, weeping, and pleading from the crowd increased as the robed victims stood facing what all believed would be the end of life.

The Angels of Light staged above the tent respond to instructions from Michael the Archangel.

EMBRACE THE SAINTS.

Angels of Light descend in pairs and placed themselves on each side of the robed victims. Although unseen, their presence was felt as fear melted away and the warm embrace of the Father's love washed over them. The sounds of taunting and weeping from the crowd also faded away replaced by beautiful Angelic singing that only they and the Angels could hear.

One by one they were ushered to the center of the arena by a black robed Capitia facilitator. As the blade was released, an Angel of Light swooped down from the perimeter and swept the freed spirit up and away in a dazzling spiral into the Heavens to a place especially prepared for them.

CHAPTER 69

Legion Headquarters, Albuquerque, NM

The chain links of their leg and wrist restraints rattle against metal as Chet and Bruce were shoved backward onto the cold steel bench. Both were blindfolded and gagged with their wrists handcuffed behind their backs. Although blindfolded, they recognized the unique sound of a modulated voice being broadcast from an Enforcer's suit.

"I have in my hand a warrant for the capture and transportation of two dissident men wanted for hijacking, theft, destruction of Capitia property, and colluding with anti-Capitia gangs. I am confident that it is you."

Two Enforcers standing behind them reached down, grabbed their handcuffed wrists, and yanked them to their feet. Bruce heard Chet's muffled growl and wanted to take action but could not. The gut-wrenching anger of powerlessness was unfamiliar and unwanted.

"You are scheduled for interrogation at Capitia Supreme Headquarters in Phoenix, Arizona."

The Enforcers behind them moved forward and yanked the blindfolds from their eyes. Before them sat the Enforcer, who had read the warrant and who had ordered them to stand by a hand signal to the Enforcers behind them. The all-gray room had no windows and but three pieces of furniture; the steel bench and the gray desk and chair of the Enforcer.

"Get them out of my sight!"

One Enforcer opened the only door and the other pushed them from behind. The leg restraints limited their leg motion resulting in stutter-steps as they made their way through the short hall to the exit door. The Enforcer in the lead stopped, knelt down, and removed their leg restraints.

"Now get moving, we don't got all day."

As the door to the outside opened, they could see the gray prisoner van waiting to take them to Phoenix. The engine was running with driver's door and rear doors standing open. One Enforcer ordered them to stop and face the rear opening as other walked toward the driver's door. To their surprise the wrist restraints were also removed before being ordered to step through the rear door into the van.

The van's interior was made for transporting prisoners including foot, wrist, and neck restraints built into the metal benches along the side walls. The cab was separated from the rear by a heavy chain-link divider secured to the driver's and passenger's seats with a narrow chain-like hatch between the seats.

Bruce pulled off the gag, leaned toward Chet, and whispered, "Hang onto something. I think they plan to throw us around back here."

No sooner had he finished speaking when the van lurched forward followed by an aggressive left turn. Chet had grabbed hold of the wrist restraints, and Bruce hung onto the chain-link divider. The aggressive swerving, acceleration, and slowing continued until they pulled onto Westbound Interstate 40.

Chet pulled off his gag and moved to sit beside Bruce. "Looks like we're are going back to the Freedom Clan."

Bruce nodded and smiled. "Could be."

He leaned close to Chet and whispered. "Remember those kill switches on the back of the suits?"

Chet looked in the direction of the cab and nodded in the affirmative.

Bruce's facial expression became stern and focused. "If you sit over there and I sit over here...and if we can time it, we can take these guys out with the push of a button."

Chet looked at the dimple that covered the kill-switch on the neck of the driver's suit. "Let's do this."

Epilogue

The battle for world domination spread like a devouring cancer. The Earth became a hunting field and the cities became prisons. Seemingly unabated, Capitia strived to achieve One World Order and the absolute power over humanity it craved.

Yet there are those whose who had read and stood on the words recorded thousands of years ago.

"Have I not commanded you? Be strong and courageous. Do not be afraid; do not be discouraged, for the LORD your God will be with you wherever you go" (Josh. 1:9 NIV).

About the Author

R. Hilary Adcock has been blessed with a full and adventurous life.

He enjoys life experiences driven by his passion for teaching, travel, aviation, sailing, architecture, and writing. His writing includes novels, poetry, and devotionals.

Paramount to his work is his devotion to God and all that God has created.

His goal for those who read his work is that they too will come to see and experience the wonder and miracle of life itself.

9 781098 058548